TALES FROM BOHEMIA

KAREL J. ERBEN

TALES FROM

BOHEMIA

*

Illustrations by Artuš Scheiner
Translated by Vera Gissing

Purnell

A PURNELL BOOK

© Albatros Publishers, Prague
Illustrations © Artuš Scheiner 1969
English text © Macdonald & Company (Publishers) Ltd

First published in Great Britain in 1987
by Macdonald & Company (Publishers) Ltd
A BPCC plc company

Printed and bound in Czechoslovakia

Macdonald & Company (Publishers) Ltd
Greater London House
Hampstead Road
London NW1 7QX

British Library Cataloguing in Publication Data

Erben K. J.
Tales from Bohemia
1. Title
891.8'634 (J) PZ8.1

ISBN 0-361-07466-2

CONTENTS

THE FIREBIRD AND THE CLEVER VIXEN

There was a king who had a most beautiful garden filled with many rare trees. In the centre of the garden stood the rarest tree of all — an apple tree, which bore just a single apple every day. But it was a very special golden apple. Each morning, the blossom turned to fruit which grew throughout the day until, by nightfall, it was ripe. The next day, another blossom appeared and an apple formed. Yet none of the ripe, golden apples ever lasted for more than a day, they always disappeared from the tree during the night. No one knew where they went to or how and this caused the king much grief.

One day, he called his eldest son to him and said, 'My son, I want you to guard the apple tree tonight. If you find out who is stealing my apples, I shall reward you most generously, and if you are clever enough to catch the thief, I shall give you half my kingdom.'

With his sword at his waist and his crossbow on his shoulder and a few sharp arrows tucked under his belt, the prince went out into the garden at dusk to keep watch. He sat down under the apple tree and waited. Before very long a terrible drowsiness came over him, and try as he might, he just could not keep awake. His hands sank into the grass, his eyes closed and soon he was dead to the world until the next morning. When he awoke, the apple was gone.

'Well,' asked the king, 'did you see the thief?'

'There was no thief, father,' the prince replied. 'The apple disappeared all by itself.'

The king shook his head in disbelief and turned to his second son. 'You keep watch tonight,' he said, 'and if you see the thief, you will be richly rewarded.'

So the second prince, armed like the first, went to keep guard. But soon he, too, fell into a deep sleep, just like his elder brother had done, and when he woke up, the apple was gone.

The next morning, when the king asked who had taken the apple, the prince replied, 'No one took it. The apple disappeared all by itself.'

'Oh, father,' cried the youngest prince, 'please let me keep watch tonight. I want to find out if the golden apple will vanish from me too!'

'My dear child,' the king replied, 'you are so young and inexperienced. What chance have you to succeed where your older brothers have failed! But if you want to keep guard over the golden apple, then do.'

That evening, as darkness fell, the youngest prince went into the

garden. He, too, armed himself with a sword, a crossbow and some arrows, but he also brought a hedgehog's skin. The prince sat down under the apple tree and spread the skin over his lap, and whenever sleep came over him, his hands fell right on top of the prickly skin and he came to with a start.

At midnight, a golden bird flew into the garden and landed on the apple tree. It was just about to snatch the apple with its beak, when the prince aimed his crossbow and let the arrow fly. It hit the bird in the wing. Though the bird got away one of its golden feathers fell to the ground, and the apple remained on the tree.

'Well, did you catch the thief?' the king asked in the morning.

'No, father,' the prince replied. 'But what is not today, may be so tomorrow. For the time being, I only have a piece of his coat.'

Then he presented the golden feather to his father and told him what had happened. The king was delighted with the feather; it was so beautiful and shone so brightly that at night no other lights were needed in the king's chambers. The courtiers, who understood such matters, said that the feather came from the Firebird and that it was more precious than all the king's treasures.

From that day, the Firebird did not return to the king's garden, and the apples no longer vanished. But the golden fruit no longer pleased the king, for he yearned to possess the Firebird. He thought of it day and night and was plunged into the deepest gloom, until his heart was sick with grief.

One day, he called his three sons to him and said, 'You can see that I am growing weaker day by day, yet I know for certain my heart would recover if I could but hear the Firebird sing. The one who brings the Firebird to sing for me will get half my kingdom at once and the rest after my death.'

The three sons immediately prepared for the journey. They bade

their father goodbye and rode in search of the Firebird. After a while, they entered a forest where the path branched into three.

'Which way shall we go?' asked the eldest.

'There are three of us and we have three paths to choose from,' replied the second. 'Let us each take a different path, then we are more likely to find the Firebird.'

'You two choose the paths you wish to follow,' the youngest suggested. 'I shall take the one that is left.'

The brothers were content with this and each chose a path. Then one of them said, 'Let us leave some kind of sign here, so that whoever returns first will know how the others have fared. Let us each plant a twig in the ground. If one grows, it will be a sign that the one who planted it has found the Firebird.'

The brothers liked this idea, and each planted a twig by the side of his chosen path and rode off.

The eldest brother rode along his path until he came to a hill. He jumped off his horse and left him to graze, whilst he himself sat on the grass. Then he unwrapped the food he had with him and began to eat.

At that moment, a little vixen came up to him. 'Oh please, oh please, young man,' she pleaded, 'I am so hungry! Give me something to eat!'

But the prince was already holding his crossbow and he shot an arrow after her. He did not see whether he missed or not, for the vixen had vanished.

The same thing happened to the second brother. As soon as he made himself comfortable in a meadow and took out his lunch, up came the hungry vixen, begging for a morsel. The moment he released his arrow, she disappeared.

The youngest brother rode on until he came to a stream. He was tired and hungry, so he leapt from his horse and flung himself on the grassy bank to eat and rest. Just as he started eating, he noticed the little red vixen. She crept nearer and nearer till, at last, she came to a stop not far from where he sat. 'Oh please, oh please, young gentleman,' she pleaded again, 'I am so hungry! Please give me something to eat!'

The prince threw her a piece of smoked meat and said, 'Come here, little red vixen! Don't be afraid of me. Why, you are hungrier than I! There is enough for both of us today.' He divided the food into two portions, one for himself and one for the vixen.

When the little red vixen had had her fill, she said, 'You have fed me well, so I shall serve you well. Mount your horse and follow me. If you do as I tell you, the Firebird shall be yours.'

She ran along in front, clearing the way with her bushy red tail; she swept away mountains, filled in deep gullies and built bridges over rivers and lakes. The prince galloped behind her until they came to a castle made of brass.

'The Firebird is in that castle,' said the vixen. 'You must enter at noon, when the guards will be asleep. Do not stop on the way. You will pass through a hall with twelve black birds in golden cages, then through a second hall with twelve golden birds in wooden cages. In the third hall the Firebird will be sitting on its perch. You will see two cages, one golden, one wooden. Do not put the bird in the golden cage, choose the wooden one, or you will be sorry.'

The prince entered the brass castle and found everything as the vixen had described. In the third hall the Firebird was sitting on its perch and it seemed to be asleep. The bird was so magnificent that the prince's heart rejoiced. He picked it up carefully and put it in the wooden cage, but then he changed his mind. 'They just don't go together,' he muttered to himself, 'this beautiful bird and that wretched cage. The Firebird belongs in the golden one!' And he took the bird out of the wooden cage and placed it in the golden one.

At that moment the Firebird woke up and started to screech, and

straightaway all the birds from both the first two halls joined in, screeching and whistling, till they awoke all the guards at the gate. The guards rushed in, seized the prince and led him to their king, who was very angry.

'Who are you, thief,' he cried, 'you, who have dared to sneak past all my guards to steal my Firebird?'

'I am no thief,' the prince said in defence, 'but I have come for the thief you are sheltering! We have an apple tree in our royal garden which bears one golden apple a day. And every night your Firebird came to steal it. Now my father the king has fallen gravely ill, his heart is failing and he will not recover unless he hears your Firebird sing. So I beg you, give me the bird.'

.'You can have it,' the king replied, 'providing you bring me Horse Golden Mane in return.'

'Why didn't you do as you were told?' the vixen asked angrily. 'You shouldn't have touched the golden cage.'

'I know I made a mistake,' the prince admitted. 'Please don't be cross with me and tell me if you know anything about Horse Golden Mane.'

'I certainly do,' the little red vixen replied, 'and I will help you find it. Now mount and follow me.'

Once again she ran in front, clearing the way with her bushy tail, the prince following at a gallop till they suddenly came upon a silver castle.

'You will find Horse Golden Mane in this castle,' the vixen said. 'Go in at noon, when the guards will be sleeping, and do not stop on the way. You will pass through a stable with twelve black horses with gold bridles, then through a second stable with twelve white horses with black bridles. In the third stable you will find Horse Golden Mane. Hanging on the wall you will see two bridles, a gold one and a leather one. Now I warn you. Leave the gold bridle alone and take the leather one, or you will be sorry!'

The prince entered the castle and found everything just as the vixen had described. In the third stable Horse Golden Mane was standing by a silver trough, eating real fire. The prince could not take his eyes off the magnificent beast. He took the leather bridle from the wall and put it on the horse, who stood there, gentle as a lamb. Then the prince saw a beautiful gold bridle set with precious stones and he admired it very much. 'How badly they go together, this magnificent horse and that ugly bridle,' he said to himself. 'Horse Golden Mane must have the gold bridle!' And he replaced the leather bridle with the gold one.

No sooner was this done, than the horse began to rear wildly and neigh loudly and straightaway all the horses in the first two stables joined in, bucking and neighing and kicking, until they woke all the guards at the gate: The guards rushed in, seized the prince and led him to their king.

'Who are you, thief,' the king stormed, 'you, who have dared to sneak past my guards to steal my Horse Golden Mane?'

'I am no thief,' the prince replied, 'I don't even want your horse, yet I must have it.'

And he explained all that had happened, and how the king of the brass castle refused to part with the Firebird unless he was given Horse Golden Mane in exchange, and he begged the king to let him have it.

'You shall have the horse,' said the king, 'providing you bring me the Golden Princess from the golden castle in the Black Sea.'

The little red vixen was waiting for the prince in the forest. When she saw him coming without the horse, she turned on him angrily. 'Didn't I warn you not to touch the gold bridle, but to take the leather one instead? Working with you is indeed a thankless task. How can I help a man who refuses to follow advice!'

'Don't be angry, little red vixen,' pleaded the prince. 'I admit I was wrong, but please help me again, just this once!'

'Just this once and never again,' the vixen agreed, 'and if you do as I tell you, you still have a chance to put everything right. Now mount your horse and follow me!'

Then the vixen ran on ahead, clearing the way with her bushy tail until they came to the golden castle in the Black Sea. 'The sea queen rules in this castle,' the vixen explained. 'She has three daughters. The Golden Princess is the youngest. Go to the queen and ask her to give you one of her daughters for a wife. If she asks you to choose your bride, pick the one who is the most simply dressed.'

The sea queen greeted the prince courteously, and when he told her why he had come, she led him to the room where her three daughters sat spinning. They were so alike that no one in the world could have told them apart, and so beautiful that the prince gasped in admiration. Each princess had a scarf wound round her head, so the colour of her hair could not be seen, and each was dressed differently. The scarf and the dress of the first were embroidered in gold, and she was spinning with a gold distaff; the second princess had a scarf and a dress embroidered in silver, and she held a silver distaff; but the third wore only a plain white scarf on her head, a simple white dress, and she was spinning with an ordinary distaff.

'Choose the one you want,' said the queen, and the prince pointed to the maiden dressed in white. 'This one is for me!' he said.

'How strange,' said the queen, who was taken by surprise. 'You couldn't have known. You must wait until tomorrow!'

The prince was so worried he did not sleep a wink that night, and at the break of dawn he was already strolling in the castle gardens. Suddenly the princess dressed in white stood before him. 'If you want to recognise me today,' she whispered, 'look out for the little fly buzzing round my head.' Then she vanished as mysteriously as she had come.

That afternoon the queen led the prince back to the room where her daughters were. 'If you can pick out the one whom you chose yesterday,' she said, 'she shall be yours. If you do not recognise her, you will lose your head.'

The three maidens stood side by side. They were all exactly alike,

and beautifully dressed in expensive clothes, and all three had golden hair so dazzling that the prince was quite blinded by the brilliance. When his eyes grew accustomed to the glare, he noticed a small golden fly buzzing round one of the maidens.

'This maiden is mine,' he said, 'she is my chosen one.'

The queen was most annoyed at this, and she said, 'You cannot win her so easily. Tomorrow I shall set you another task.'

So, the next morning, she took the prince to the window, gave him a small, golden sieve and said, pointing to a huge lake near the forest, 'If you can drain the lake with this sieve by nightfall, the Golden Princess will be yours. But if you fail, you shall lose your head.'

The prince walked sadly to the lake, the sieve in his hand. He plunged it into the water, but the moment he lifted it out, all the water trickled out again. It was useless! With a sigh he sat down on the bank, the sieve beside him, wondering what to do.

Suddenly the white maiden reappeared and said, 'Why are you so sad?'

'How can I be otherwise,' the prince replied, 'seeing that I shall never win you. Your mother has set me an impossible task.'

'Stop worrying,' the princess soothed him. 'It can be done.' She took the sieve and tossed it into the middle of the lake. Then all at once, the water began to boil and thick clouds came from the lake and hung so low on the ground that the prince could not see his hand in front of his face.

Just then, he heard a sound of hooves behind him and when he turned round, there was the horse and the little red vixen. 'Quick!' she cried, 'mount your horse at once with your maiden, and ride for your life!'

The Horse flew like an arrow back along the path the vixen had cleared when they came. This time she ran at the rear and with her bushy tail she swept away bridges, hollowed out gullies and rebuilt mountains, leaving everything as it was before. The prince was overjoyed that he had won the Golden Princess, but he hated the thought of having to part from her. The nearer they came to the silver castle, the more slowly he rode and the sadder he grew.

'You are sad at having to give the Golden Princess to the king of the silver castle in exchange for Horse Golden Mane, aren't you?' asked the vixen. 'I have helped you through a lot, and I won't desert you now.' She jumped over a fallen tree, turned a somersault and, instead of a red vixen, there stood a golden-haired maiden, exactly like the one on the horse. 'Leave the princess here in the forest,' she said, 'and take me to the king in the silver castle, then he will let you keep

Horse Golden Mane. When he is yours, ride away with your princess.'

The king was very thrilled with the golden-haired maiden, and readily gave the prince Horse Golden Mane and the gold bridle as well. Then he held a magnificent feast in honour of his bride to which he invited all the noblemen. When they had drunk their fill and were feeling merry, the king asked his guests what they thought of his bride.

'She is lovely,' said one of the noblemen, 'she could not be lovelier. But it seems to me that she has the eyes of a vixen.'

The moment he said that word, the golden-haired maiden turned into a vixen again and shot through the door like a flash. She followed the prince and the Golden Princess, destroying with her tail the path she had made on her way out. She swept away bridges, hollowed out gullies and rebuilt mountains, leaving everything as it was before. By the time she caught up with the prince and the princess, they were close to the brass castle where the Firebird was kept.

'Your Golden Princess looks so lovely on Horse Golden Mane,' the vixen said to the prince. 'Are you not sorry that you must give up the horse to get the Firebird?'

'Of course I am sorry for the princess's sake and mine,' the prince replied, 'but I am glad for my father's sake, for the Firebird will make him well.'

'The Golden Princess and Horse Golden Mane and the Firebird shall stay together,' the vixen vowed. 'I have helped you through a lot, and I shall help you this time, too.' With that she jumped over a fallen tree, turned a somersault and, instead of a vixen, there stood another golden-maned horse identical to the one the prince and the princess were riding.

'Take me to the brass castle,' she said, so that the king may give

you the Firebird in exchange for me. When the bird is yours, ride like the wind!'

The king was very pleased to have the golden-maned horse and readily gave the prince the Firebird in exchange, and the gold cage as well. Then he invited many noblemen to show off the horse, and he asked them what they thought of it.

'It is a magnificent animal,' said one of the noblemen. 'It could hardly be more magnificent, but it seems to me it has the tail of a fox.'

No sooner had he spoken, than the golden-maned horse turned into a vixen again and shot through the gate like lightning. She followed the prince and the Golden Princess, destroying with her tail the path she had made on their way out. She swept away bridges, hollowed out gullies and rebuilt mountains, leaving everything as it was before. She caught up with them by the side of the stream where she had first met the prince.

'Now the Firebird is yours,' she said, 'and much else besides. You do not need me any more. Ride home in peace and do not stop on the way, or you will be sorry.' With that she vanished.

The prince rode on, in his hand the Firebird in its golden cage, Horse Golden Mane trotting beside him and the Golden Princess on the horse's back, holding the jewelled bridle. When they came to the crossing where the prince had parted from his brothers, he remembered the twigs each of them had planted at the side of their chosen path. The twigs of his brothers were withered, but his had grown into a fine, leafy tree. The prince was delighted to see this, and as both he and the princess were very tired after such a long journey, they decided to rest under the tree. The prince leapt from his horse, helped the Golden Princess from hers, then tethered both horses to the tree and hung the cage with the Firebird on one of the branches. Before very long they were overcome by drowsiness and were soon fast a-sleep.

While they slept, the prince's two brothers returned to the crossing, both from opposite sides and both with empty hands. First they noticed that their twigs were withered, but that their youngest brother's twig had grown into a beautiful tree. Then they saw their brother sleeping soundly under the tree, the lovely Golden Princess beside him, Horse Golden Mane nearby, and the Firebird hanging above them in its golden cage.

It was then that evil thoughts were born in their hearts and one said to the other, 'Now father will give our brother half his kingdom, and will make him his successor when he dies. We had better kill him. You can keep the Golden Princess, I shall keep Horse Golden Mane, and we will give the Firebird to our father to sing for him. The kingdom we can divide evenly between us.'

It was no sooner said than done. They cut their youngest brother's body up into many pieces, and they threatened the Golden Princess with death if she told the truth.

When they arrived home, the brothers put Horse Golden Mane in a marble stable, the Firebird in the king's bedroom and the Golden Princess in a beautiful chamber with many ladies to wait upon her.

The sick old king looked at the Firebird and asked his sons whether they had any news of his youngest son.

'No news at all,' the brothers lied. 'He must have perished somewhere.'

The old king remained as sad as ever. The Firebird did not sing, Horse Golden Mane mournfully hung its head and the Golden Princess spoke not a word, nor did she ever comb her golden hair, but she wept unceasingly.

The little vixen came upon the body of the youngest prince, all cut into little pieces. She gathered them all up and placed each in its proper place, and she vainly tried to bring the prince to life again. Suddenly, she noticed a raven with her two young ones hovering over the prince's dead body. The vixen hid in the grass under a bush, and when one of the young ravens settled on the body, she sprang out, seized the bird and pretended she was about to tear it apart.

The terrified mother raven flew to the vixen and begged, 'Don't eat my poor child, it has done nothing to hurt you! Let it go and I will help you whenever you need me.'

'I need you now,' said the vixen. 'Bring me the water of life and of death from the Black Sea, and I will let your young one go.'

The raven flew away, promising to bring the two waters. It flew three days and nights, and when it returned it was carrying two fish bladders filled with water: one contained the water of life, the other the water of death. The vixen took the bladders and tore the young raven in half. Then she laid the two halves side by side and sprinkled them with the water of death and in a trice, they grew together again. Then she sprinkled the young raven's body with the water of life, and the bird flapped its wings and flew away. The vixen now sprinkled the water of death over the prince's body which was all in little pieces, and at once it was whole again, there was not even a single scar. Then she sprinkled it with the water of life. The prince awoke, as if from a dream, staggered to his feet, yawned and said, 'I've slept like the dead!'

'You have indeed!' the vixen agreed, 'and if it weren't for me you would have stayed sleeping for ever. Didn't I warn you to ride straight home and not to stop on the way?' And she told him all that had happened. Then she went with him to the edge of the forest near the royal castle and before parting, she handed the prince a worn suit of a servant. 'Put it on,' she said, 'it will help you.' And with that she vanished.

The prince did as he was bid and dressed in the rough clothes, he went to the castle. He was taken on as a stable boy and nobody recognised him.

Sometime later, the prince overheard two grooms. 'Isn't it a shame about that lovely Horse Golden Mane, he is so lifeless and won't eat a thing,' one groom said. 'If he goes on like this, he will surely die,' added the other.

The prince picked a handful of stringy old pea pods and said to the grooms, 'I'll lay a bet with you that the horse will eat these at once.'

'What a joke!' the grooms laughed. 'Even our plough horses wouldn't touch such rubbish.'

Nevertheless they followed the prince into the marble stable. The prince stroked the horse's golden mane and said, 'Why are you so sad, my horse Golden Mane!'

The horse recognised the voice of his master and he flung up his head, neighed joyfully and tucked into the old pea pods. The news that the new stable boy had cured Horse Golden Mane spread quickly through the castle until it reached the ears of the king. The king sent for him at once.

'I hear that you have cured Horse Golden Mane,' he said. 'Could you cure the Firebird and make it sing? The bird is so sad, it sits there with drooping wings and will not eat. If it dies, I shall die too.'

'Have no fear, great king,' said the prince, 'the Firebird will not die. Please have some barley husks brought here. Not only will the bird eat them but it will cheer up and sing.'

'What a joke!' the servants roared. 'The idea of the Firebird eating such trash! Why, even our geese wouldn't touch it!' But the servants fetched the barley husks and the prince scattered them over the floor of the cage, stroked the bird's golden plumage and said, 'Why are you so sad, my Firebird?'

The bird knew the prince at once by his voice, and it began to hop about happily, shaking its coat, smoothing down its feathers and pecking away at the barley husks all at the same time. Then it burst into song and sang so wondrously that the heart of the old sick king began to mend. And as the Firebird sang, the king grew stronger and stronger, till he rose from his bed completely cured and joyfully embraced the unknown stable boy.

'If only we could help the lovely Golden Princess,' the king then said. 'She speaks not a word and she never combs her beautiful golden hair, nor does a morsel of food pass her lips. But she weeps unceasingly.'

31

'Leave the princess to me, my king,' the stable boy suggested. 'Perhaps I shall be able to cheer her up.'

The king led him to the sad princess and the prince took her white hand in his and said, 'Why are you so sad, my bride?'

The princess then recognised him and flung her arms around his neck, crying for joy.

The king was astonished at what he was seeing and hearing, until the prince turned to him and said, 'Father! Don't you recognise your own youngest son? It was not my brothers, but I who won the Firebird, Horse Golden Mane and the lovely Golden Princess!'

Then the prince told his father all that had happened, and the princess added that the brothers threatened her with death, should she betray them. The two elder brothers just stood there and, knowing that they were doomed, shook like leaves, unable to utter a word.

The furious king showed no mercy and ordered their execution at once.

When that was over, the young prince married his beautiful, golden-haired bride. And, as he had promised, the old king gave them half his kingdom straightaway, and the other half after his death.

THE WOODEN BABY

There was once a man and his wife who lived in an old cottage at the edge of a village close to the forest. The husband worked now and then as a hired hand and the wife spun flax to sell. Poor as they were they longed for a little son.

'You should be glad God has not sent you one,' the village folk said. 'You barely have enough to keep body and soul together as it is.'

But this did not stop the poor couple yearning. 'If the two of us can keep alive, we could surely manage to feed a small baby,' they reasoned. 'If only we were blessed with one!'

One morning when the husband was chopping wood in the forest, he dug out a tree stump which was shaped like a baby. It had a head,

33

body, arms and legs. All he needed to do was to round and smooth the head and scoop out little holes for the eyes. When he had trimmed the small roots on the hands and feet to make them look like fingers and toes, the stump was just like a real baby, except it did not cry.

The man took the stump home and gave it to his wife. 'Here is what you have always wanted — a baby boy!'

The wife wrapped the wooden baby in a little feather quilt, rocked it in her arms and sang,

> 'Rock-a-bye baby,
> My darling boy.
> Are you a real son,
> Or only a toy?
>
> When you awake
> From your slumber, my sweet,
> Mama shall give you
> Some good food to eat.
> Hush-a-bye baby,
> My love and my joy.'

Suddenly, the baby began to wriggle under the quilt and, to the woman's amazement, he opened his eyes and cried, 'I am so hungry, Mother!'

The woman was so delighted, she jumped for joy. She tucked the baby in her bed and hurried to cook some food. As soon as it was ready, the wooden baby gobbled it all up and began to shout again, 'I am still hungry, Mother!'

There was not a morsel of food left in the cottage, so the woman

cried, 'Wait, little one, wait! I'll be back in a minute,' and she ran to her neighbour and brought back a jug full of milk.

The wooden baby downed it in one gulp and screamed for more.

'Well I never!' said the astonished mother. 'Haven't you had enough yet?' But she went to the village and borrowed a loaf of bread. She left it on the table whilst she went out to fetch water to make some broth. The mother had hardly left the room when the wooden baby, seeing the bread on the table, wriggled out of the quilt, jumped on to the bench and, in a flash, the loaf was gone and he was screaming again, 'Mother, I want more to eat!'

The mother came in to cut the bread for the soup, she looked for it, but it was gone! In the corner stood her wooden baby as fat as a barrel, rolling his eyes at her.

'God preserve us, boy, surely you haven't eaten the whole loaf?'

'Yes, I did, Mother, and now I'll eat you too!' With that he opened his mouth wide and swallowed her whole.

Shortly afterwards his father returned. The minute he set foot inside the door, the wooden baby was shouting, 'I am so hungry, Father!'

The man couldn't believe his eyes. There was his son, his stomach like a barrel, his mouth like the entrance to a forge, rolling his eyes. 'Lord have mercy on us!' he whispered, then stammered, 'Where is your mother?'

'I have eaten her — and I'll eat you too!' And the wooden baby opened his mouth and in a trice his father was inside him.

But the more he ate, the greedier he grew. As there was nothing left in the cottage to eat, he staggered towards the village. He met a dairymaid pushing a wheelbarrow full of clover.

'Whatever have you eaten to get that gigantic tummy?' she asked. The wooden baby replied,

> *'I've gobbled and gobbled*
> *All that I can;*
> *A jugful of milk*
> *And food from the pan.*
> *A whole loaf of bread*
> *And, in less than a wink,*
> *Mum and Dad, too.*
> *So now, let me think . . .*
> *I will eat you!'*

Then, he sprang forward, and the dairymaid and the wheelbarrow joined the others inside his stomach.

In a little while, he met a peasant, his cart heaped with hay. The wooden baby barred his way, and the horse came to a halt.

'Move out of the way, you little monster!' the peasant shouted. 'If I get hold of you, I'll . . .' And he cracked his whip threateningly.

But the wooden baby took no notice and began again,

> *'I've gobbled and gobbled*
> *All that I can;*
> *A jugful of milk*
> *And food from the pan.*
> *A whole loaf of bread*
> *And, in less than a wink,*
> *My Mum and Dad, too*
> *And a dairymaid, think!*
> *But, as I'm still hungry . . .*
> *I will eat you!'*

Before the peasant knew what was happening he, too, found himself inside the huge stomach, horse, cart and all!

The wooden baby wobbled on. He saw a field where a swineherd was tending his pigs. He licked his lips and snapped up the lot. There was not a trace left to show they had ever existed. Then he rolled downhill to the foot of a mountain and there he saw a shepherd with a flock of sheep.

'As I've eaten so much, I may as well enjoy these too,' the wooden baby muttered, and he stuffed them all inside him — the sheep, the shepherd and even Watch, the sheepdog. Then he staggered to another field, where an old woman was hoeing cabbages. Without thinking twice about it, he pulled out the plants one by one and tucked into them.

'Stop damaging my field,' the old woman cried crossly. 'You've had more than plenty to eat, you can't want more!'

The wooden baby sneered at her and said,

> *'I've gobbled and gobbled*
> *All that I can;*
> *A jugful of milk*
> *And food from the pan.*
> *A whole loaf of bread*
> *And, all this is true -*
> *My Mum and my Dad*
> *And a dairymaid, too!*
> *I've eaten a peasant*
> *And all of his hay,*
> *Pigs, swineherd and shepherd*
> *And sheep, in a day.*
> *But as I'm still hungry . . .*
> *I'll eat you, if I may!'*

The wooden baby opened his mouth and tried to snap the old woman up, but she was so nimble she managed to strike him with her hoe and slice his stomach wide open. The wooden baby sank to the ground, quite dead.

You should have seen what happened then! Out jumped Watch the sheepdog, followed by the shepherd and all his sheep. Watch rounded up the herd, the shepherd blew his whistle and drove them towards their field. Next came the pigs, the swineherd behind them; he cracked his whip and followed the shepherd. Then the horse trotted out, pulling the cart loaded with hay. The peasant picked up the reins, swore under his breath and drove off towards the village. The dairymaid, pushing her wheelbarrow, followed the cart. The mother and father of the wooden baby ran out last of all. They ran for their lives back to the old cottage, the borrowed loaf of bread tucked under the woman's arm.

So, the man and his wife lived happily for the rest of their days and never once wished for a baby!

COOK, MUG, COOK!

Once there was a poor widow who lived in a village with her daughter. All they possessed was an old cottage with a leaky roof and a handful of hens in the attic. During the winter the mother gathered wood in the forest and in the summer she picked woodland berries, whilst in the autumn she scrounged what she could from the fields. The girl collected the eggs which the hens laid in the attic and took them to the town market to sell. This is how they survived.

One summer's day the mother fell ill, so the daughter had to go to the forest to pick berries, as they had nothing to eat at home. She took an empty pot with her and a slice of black bread. When the pot was full, the girl sat down beside a well to rest and to eat her bread. It was exactly midday.

Suddenly an old woman appeared, dressed in rags like a beggar. In her hand she held an empty mug.

'Oh, my dear girl,' the old woman sighed, 'how I should like something to eat! Not a single morsel has passed my lips these last two days. Could you spare me a piece of your bread?'

'Why not?' the girl replied readily, 'have all of it, please do! I only hope you won't find it too hard to swallow.'

With that she gave the old beggar woman all her lunch.

'Lord be praised, my girl, Lord be praised!' the old woman cried. 'As you have shown such kindness to me, I will give you something, too. Here, take this mug. When you get home, put it on the table and say, "Cook, mug, cook!" and it will cook as much semolina pudding as you wish. When you have enough, simply say, "Stop, mug, stop!" and it will stop cooking. But do not forget these words.'

With that the old woman handed the mug over and disappeared.

When the girl returned home, she told her mother what had happened in the forest, and she placed the mug on the table and commanded, 'Cook, mug, cook!' to see whether the old woman had been telling the truth. And wonder of wonders! Semolina pudding rose from the base of the mug, bubbling and growing, and before one could count up to ten, the mug was overflowing.

'Stop, mug, stop!' the girl cried, and the mug stopped at once.

Mother and daughter sat down and tucked in with relish. The pudding was quite delicious.

After their meal, the girl put some eggs in a basket and went to the market. But no one wanted to pay the price she asked for the eggs, and it was dusk by the time she managed to sell them.

43

The widow sat at home, longingly gazing at the magic mug, for she was hungry again. 'I don't have to wait,' she thought in the end, and placing the mug on the table, she commanded, 'Cook, mug, cook!' And again the semolina pudding began to bubble and grow, and before the woman turned around, the mug was full.

'I must fetch a dish and a spoon,' the widow muttered and went to the scullery.

When she returned, she nearly died of fright. Thick semolina pudding was pouring from the mug on to the table, from the table to the bench and from the bench to the floor. For the life of her, the mother could not remember how to stop the mug making more semolina pudding.

She slammed the dish over the mug, but that was no good. The dish fell to the floor and broke into tiny pieces, and out poured the semolina, just like a white flood.

There was so much of it in the kitchen, that the woman had to escape to the bedroom. She wrung her hands and lamented, 'Oh, what an evil gift my unfortunate daughter has brought home! I thought right from the start it would do us no good!'

By now the semolina was pouring out of the kitchen into the bedroom; the pile grew thicker and higher by the minute.

The mother was at her wits end, so she climbed to the attic, sobbing and lamenting ceaselessly.

The semolina mountain grew and grew, and before long it was rolling out of the cottage door and windows like thick white clouds, flooding the road and piling up on the village square. Goodness knows where it would have ended, had the daughter not returned and commanded, 'Stop, mug, stop!'

But by now there was such a great pile of pudding covering the square, that when the farmers were returning from the fields that night, they had no option but to eat their way through that mountain of semolina in order to get to their homes.

It took three whole days for the villagers to clear away all the semolina and after that, the daughter took good care to look after the mug herself. You may be sure she never forgot those magic words, 'Stop, mug, stop!'

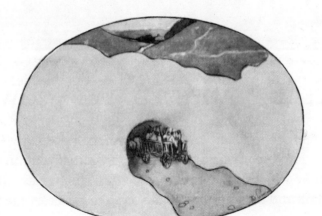

WATERBOY AND OLD MAN KNOWALL

Maybe it really happened and maybe not, but the story has it that once long ago there was a king in Bohemia who loved hunting. One day, when he was chasing deer in the forest, he lost his way. It was growing dark and the king was all alone, so he was very glad when he came upon a lonely cottage in a clearing. It was the home of a miner.

'Can you lead me out of the forest?' asked the king. 'I shall pay you handsomely.'

'I'd go with you gladly,' the miner replied, 'but as you see my wife is heavy with child and is expecting the baby tonight. I cannot leave her. But how far do you think you would get in the dark? Why don't you bed for the night on the soft hay in our loft, then in the morning I'll show you the way.'

Soon afterwards the miner's baby son was born. The king, above in the loft, was unable to sleep. At midnight he noticed a strange glow in the room below him. He peeped through a crack in the floorboards and saw the miner in a deep sleep, and the wife lying there deathly pale and lifeless. Beside the baby's cradle stood three old women, all in white, each with a candle in her hand. They were the Three Fates.

The first said, 'My gift to this boy is that he shall face many perils.'

The second said, 'My gift to this boy is that he shall come safely through them and will live to a ripe old age.'

The third said, 'My gift is that of a bride born this night to the wife of the king who sleeps in the loft above.' The Three Fates blew out their candles and all was dark and still.

The king felt as if a sword had been plunged into his breast. He did not close an eye the whole night long and racked his brains how to prevent what had been prophesied from coming to pass.

When morning came, the baby began to cry. The miner rose and saw that during the night his wife had fallen into an eternal sleep.

'Oh, my poor little orphan,' he lamented, 'what shall I do with you now!'

'Give the child to me,' said the king, seizing his chance. 'I shall care for him well and I will give you so much money that you will never need work again to your dying day.'

The miner was delighted and the king left, promising to send for the baby very soon. When he returned to his palace, he was told the joyful news that on that very night, his wife had given birth to a beautiful daughter.

The king, his face like thunder, summoned a servant and said, 'Go into the forest to the miner's cottage, hand over this money and take away his baby. You are to drown that child on your way back. If you fail to do so, you yourself shall drink the water till you die!'

The servant did as he was bid. He carried the baby in a basket, and when he came to a foot bridge over a deep, wide river, he threw baby and basket into the water.

'Good riddance, my unwelcome son-in-law!' said the king, when the servant returned and reported that his task had been accomplished.

The king was now content, thinking that the infant had drowned. But the basket had floated safely with the current and the baby had slept soundly, rocked by the waves, till it came near a fisherman's hut.

The fisherman was sitting on a bank mending his net, when he saw a strange object bobbing up and down on the water. He jumped into his boat, rowed after the baby and pulled it out of the water.

He took the infant to his wife and said, 'You always wanted a baby son, and here he is. The river has brought him to us, so let us call him Waterboy.'

The wife was overjoyed and she brought the boy up as if he was her very own.

Time passes as the river flows, and the boy grew into a handsome youth, who had no equal far and wide. It so happened that, one summer's day, the king chanced to pass by. The day was unbearably hot, he was thirsty, so he stopped and asked the fisherman for a drink of water. When Waterboy handed it to him, the king looked him over, quite impressed.

'A fine lad you have here, fisherman,' he remarked. 'Is he your son?'

'He is and he isn't,' answered the man. 'It is twenty years to the

day since I found him float-
ing down the river as a tiny
baby, and we have brought
him up as our own.'

The king turned as white
as a sheet and his head began to spin. He realized
then that this handsome
young man was the baby he
had ordered to be drowned.
But he recovered his com-
posure at once, dismounted
and said, 'I need to send a
message to my palace and
there is no one with me.
Can your son take it?'

'Your wish is our com-
mand,' the fisherman replied. 'The boy shall go.'

The king asked for writ-
ing materials and wrote to
the queen, 'The youth who
is the bearer of this letter
must die at once. He is an
evil enemy of mine. Let it be
done before my return.
Such is my will.' Then he
folded the letter and sealed
it with his ring.

Waterboy set off at once.

His journey took him through a huge forest and he, too, lost his way. The forest was getting wilder and thicker, and darkness was falling rapidly, so he was relieved when he met an old woman.

'Where are you going, Waterboy?' she asked.

'I am taking a message to the king's palace, but I have lost my way. Can you direct me back to the path, dear lady?'

'You won't get there tonight in the dark,' said the old woman. 'Stay the night with me. You won't be under a stranger's roof, for I am your godmother.'

The youth let himself be persuaded and a few steps further on, they came upon a pretty little house, which seemed to have sprung out of the ground. That night, while Waterboy was asleep, the old woman took the letter from his pocket and replaced it with another, which said, 'The young man who brings you this letter is to marry our daughter without delay. He is my chosen son-in-law. Let this be done before my return. Such is my will.'

When the queen read the letter, she at once made preparations for the wedding. Neither she nor the princess could take their eyes off the bridegroom, so greatly was he to their liking. Waterboy, too, was more than pleased with his bride.

A few days later, the king returned and when he realised what had happened, his fury knew no bounds.

'But you yourself commanded me to hold the wedding before your return!' the queen defended herself, and handed him the letter.

The king examined the paper, the writing, the seal — they were truly those he had sent. Then he went to his son-in-law and questioned him about his journey.

Waterboy told how he had lost his way in the forest and that he had spent the night with his godmother.

'What does she look like?' asked the king.

As soon as the youth had described her, the king knew that she was the same old woman who had promised his daughter to the miner's son twenty years before.

He thought and he thought and then he said, 'What is done cannot be undone. But you cannot be my son-in-law just like that! If you wish to keep my daughter as your wife, you must bring her a dowry of three golden hairs from Old Man Knowall.' The king was sure such an impossible task would get rid of his unwanted son-in-law for ever.

Waterboy bade his bride goodbye and set off. He easily found his way, for one of the Fates was his godmother. He travelled on and on, crossing mountains and rivers, till he came to the Black Sea. There he saw a ferryman aboard his boat.

'God be with you, old man!' Waterboy said in greeting.

'May the Lord grant it be so,' said the ferryman. 'Where are you going, young traveller?'

'To Old Man Knowall for three golden hairs.'

'Ho, ho! I have waited so long for such a man as you. For twenty years now I have ferried folk across, and there is no one to free me from my task. If you promise to ask Old Man Knowall when my labour will be at an end, I will take you across.'

Waterboy promised and the ferryman ferried him across.

Next, he came to a large city, which looked shabby and sad. At the city gate he met an old man leaning on a stick and dragging himself painfully along.

'Lord give you good morrow, greybeard!'

'May the Lord grant it be so, fair youth! Where are you going?'

'To Old Man Knowall for three golden hairs.'

'Ay, ay! We have waited long for such a man as you! I must take you at once to our king.'

When they were before him, the king said, 'I hear you are going as a messenger to Old Man Knowall. We have an apple tree here, which used to bear apples of youth. Whoever ate one, even if he were at death's door, grew young again. But for twenty years now the tree has borne no fruit. Promise me you will ask Old Man Knowall what can be done, and I shall reward you royally.'

Waterboy promised and the king dismissed him graciously.

Later on, the youth came to another large city, but it lay almost in ruins. Near the city walls a son was digging a grave for his deceased father, and tears as big as peas rolled down his face.

'Lord give you good morrow, grief-stricken grave digger!' said Waterboy.

'Lord grant it be so, fair youth! Where are you going?'

'To Old Man Knowall for three golden hairs.'

'To Old Man Knowall? What a pity you didn't come sooner! Our king has waited a long time for such a man. I must take you to him.'

When they were before him, the king said, 'I hear you are going as a messenger to Old Man Knowall. We have a well here from which we used to draw the water of life. Whoever drank it, even if he were dying, was cured at once. And, if already dead, when sprinkled with this water, he would rise to his feet alive and well. But twenty years ago the well dried up. Promise me you will ask Old Man Knowall what can be done, and I shall reward you handsomely.'

Waterboy promised and the king dismissed him with his blessing.

His journey took him through a long, dark forest, in the middle of which he found a big green meadow full of flowers. In this meadow stood the golden palace of Old Man Knowall, and it glittered like fire. Waterboy entered, but found no one inside except an old woman sitting in a corner, spinning.

'Welcome, Waterboy,' she said. 'I am happy to see you again.' She was the godmother who had sheltered him the night he was carrying the king's letter. 'What brings you here?'

'The king refuses to let me be his son-in-law just like that, so he has sent me for three golden hairs of Old Man Knowall.'

The old woman laughed and said, 'Old Man Knowall happens to be my son, the bright Sun. Each morning he is just an infant, by noon a grown man and by nightfall an old man. I will get you the three golden hairs from his head, so that I too shall prove myself

worthy of being your godmother. But godson, you cannot stay here openly. My son may be a good soul, but when he returns ravenous at night, he could quite easily roast and eat you for his supper. Jump into this empty tub, I'll close the lid on top of you.'

Waterboy begged the old woman to ask Old Man Knowall the three questions he needed answering.

'I'll ask,' she said, 'and you pay attention to what he replies.'

Suddenly, the wind howled outside, the western window of the palace burst open and the Sun flew in — an old man with a golden head.

'I smell, I smell a human worm!' he growled. 'Have you someone here, mother?'

'Star of the day, how could I have someone here without you seeing him? I know what it is. You fly the whole day long over the world and your nostrils are filled with human scent. No wonder it still lingers on when you get home!'

The old man made no comment, but sat down to his supper. When he had eaten, he laid his golden head on his mother's knee and began to doze. When the old woman saw he was asleep, she pulled out one of his golden hairs and threw it on the floor. It rang like the peal of a bell.

'What do you want of me, mother?' the Sun grumbled.

'Nothing, my son, nothing. I was dozing and I had a strange dream.'

'What did you dream?'

'I dreamed about a city which had a well with the water of life. Whoever was sick and drank from it was cured, and whoever had died and was sprinkled with it, came to life again. But the well has been dry for the past twenty years. Is there any way it can be made to flow again?'

'Easily! Down in that well sits a frog blocking the spring. If the frog is killed and the well is cleaned, then the water will flow as before.'

When Old Man Knowall fell asleep again, the old woman plucked out a second golden hair and threw it to the ground.

'What is the matter this time, mother?'

'Nothing, my dear son, nothing. I was dozing and had another strange dream. I dreamed of a city where they had an apple tree which bore the apple of youth. Whoever was old and ate one, became young again. But for twenty years now the tree has borne no fruit. Can anything be done?'

'Quite easily. Under the tree lies a serpent, devouring its strength. If the serpent is killed and the tree transplanted, it will bear the fruit of youth again.'

Once again the Sun dropped off to sleep and the mother plucked out the third golden hair.

'Are you never going to let me go to sleep?' Old Man Knowall cried crossly and was about to rise.

'Lie still, my son, lie still! Do not be angry with me, I didn't mean to wake you. But I had yet another strange dream. I saw a ferryman on the Black Sea. For the past twenty years he has been ferrying folk across, and no one comes to release him. Will his labour ever end?'

'He must be the son of a foolish woman! Let him thrust the oar into another's hand and jump ashore, then that other will be the ferryman. But now let me rest. I must be off very early to dry the tears which the king of Bohemia's daughter sheds for her husband, the son of a miner, whom the king has sent for three hairs of mine.'

Just before dawn, a great wind rose outside and, instead of the old Sun, a lovely golden-haired infant awoke on the old woman's lap. This was the morning Sun, and he bade his mother goodbye and flew out through the eastern window.

The old woman now uncovered the tub and said to Waterboy, 'Here are the three golden hairs of Old Man Knowall. You already have the answers to your three questions. Go, and may God go with you. You will not see me again, for there will be no need.'

Waterboy thanked the old woman and left.

When he reached the first city, the king asked him, 'What news?'

'Good news!' Waterboy replied. 'Clean out your well and kill the frog which sits on the spring, and the water will flow as before.'

At once the king gave orders for this to be done and when he saw water gushing forth again, he gave the youth twelve horses as white as snow which he loaded with as much gold and silver and precious stones as they could carry.

When Waterboy reached the second city, the king asked, 'What news?'

'Good news!' Waterboy replied. 'Dig up the apple tree and kill the serpent you will find eating its roots. Replant the tree and it will bear fruit as before.'

At once the king gave orders for this to be done, and just in a single night the apple tree was full of the most beautiful blossom. The king was overjoyed and gave Waterboy twelve horses as black as ravens, loaded with as much riches as they could carry.

Waterboy rode on till he came to the Black Sea where the ferryman asked if he had discovered how he would be freed.

'Most certainly,' said the youth, 'but first ferry me over. Then I will tell you.'

The ferryman objected to this, but when he saw there was no other way, he ferried Waterboy across with all his riches and four and twenty horses.

Waterboy said to him then, 'Thrust the oar into the hand of the next man you are about to ferry across. Jump ashore and he will be the ferryman instead of you!'

The king could hardly believe his eyes when Waterboy returned with the three golden hairs of Old Man Knowall, and the princess wept, not with grief, but for joy at her husband's safe return.

'Where did you get these fine horses and all the riches?' marvelled the king.

'I earned them,' Waterboy said, and went on to relate how he had helped one king to obtain youth-giving apples, and another king life giving water.

'Apples of youth! Water of life!' the king murmured under his breath, 'if I ate such an apple, I would grow young, and if I died, the water would bring me to life again!'

Without delay he left to find the apples of youth and the water of life, and he has not returned to this day.

So the miner's son ruled instead of the king, just as his god-mother had predicted. As for the king, perhaps he is still ferrying folk across the Black Sea!

PRINCESS GOLDIE

A long time ago, in the ancient land of Bohemia, there lived an old woman. One day she knocked on the palace gates and asked to see the king. She looked so aged and frail, yet so wise that the guards let her in. When the old woman was alone with the king, she uncovered the basket she was carrying. Inside it was a snake.

'Let your cook prepare the snake for your table,' she said. 'Once you have eaten it, you will understand all that is said by birds of the air, beasts of the land and fish of the sea.'

The king was delighted that he would know something that nobody else knew, and without wasting time he ordered his servant, Georgie, to prepare the 'fish' for his dinner.

'Don't you dare taste that fish yourself,' he added, 'or you shall pay for it with your life!'

Georgie thought it all very strange.

'I've never seen such a fish in all my life,' he muttered to himself. 'It looks exactly like a snake! And what sort of cook would I be if I did not taste the dish I was preparing?'

When the fish was cooked, Georgie put the tiniest little bit in his mouth just to taste it. At that very moment he heard a buzzing noise close to his ear:

'Give us some too! Give us some too!'

Georgie looked round to see who was talking to him, but all he could see were a few flies buzzing about the kitchen.

Then he heard a wheezy voice shouting in the street, 'Where shall we go? Where shall we go?'

And a shriller voice answering, 'To the miller's barley field, to the miller's barley field!'

Georgie stuck his head out of the window and saw a gander with a flock of geese.

'So!' he thought, 'it's that kind of a fish!' He guessed rightly what it was all about, and quickly popped another little piece into his mouth before carrying the snake to the king.

After dinner the king said to Georgie, 'Saddle my horse, I want to go riding. Saddle yours too and come with me.'

The king rode in front and Georgie followed. As they were crossing a green meadow, Georgie's horse reared slightly and neighed, 'Oh, la la, brother, I feel so lighthearted I could jump over mountains!'

'It's alright for you,' the other horse neighed back, 'I'd like to jump too, but I have an old man on my back. If I were to leap, he'd fall off like a sack and break his neck.'

'So what? Let him!' Georgie's horse replied. 'Then you can carry a young man instead of the old boy!'

Georgie couldn't help but laugh at this conversation, quietly of course, so the king would not hear. But the king had also understood what the horses had said. He looked round and noticed the grin on Georgie's face. 'What are you grinning about?' he said.

'Oh, nothing important, Your Majesty,' Georgie lied. 'It was just a passing thought.'

Nevertheless the king was now suspicious of him, and he did not trust the horses either, so he headed back home.

When they reached the palace, the king asked Georgie to pour him out a glass of wine and to fill it right to the brim. 'You'll pay with your head,' he warned, 'if you pour a drop too little or a drop too much!'

Georgie lifted the flagon of wine and started to pour. Just then two little birds flew in through the window. The first had three golden hairs in its beak and it was being chased by the other.

'Hand them over!' the second bird chirped crossly. 'They're mine!'

'No, I won't!' cheeped the first. 'They belong to me! I picked them off the ground!'

'But I saw them fall when Goldie was combing her hair. Give me a couple at least.'

'No, not a single one!' insisted the first bird. 'They're mine, and that's that.'

The bird in pursuit then seized the free end of the golden hairs in its beak, and they both tugged and pulled and fluttered about till

62

each was left with one, while
the third hair dropped to
the floor with a tinkling
sound. All this caught
Georgie's attention and he
spilled a drop of the wine.

'You've forfeited your life
to me!' the king cried, 'but I
shall be merciful if you find
the golden-haired maiden
and bring her to me to be
my bride.'

What could Georgie do?
To save his life, he just had
to find Goldie, but he had
no idea where to look for
her. With a sigh he saddled
his horse and set off.

Presently, as he was ap-
proaching a dark forest, he
noticed a small bush burning at the side of the path.
There were sparks falling
on an anthill and ants were
rushing about, trying to escape, carrying little white
eggs on their backs.

'Oh, help us, help us!'
they pleaded. 'We are being
burnt alive, and our young
ones are still in the egg!'

Georgie leapt from his horse, cut down the bush and stamped out the fire.

'Thank you, thank you!' cried the ants. 'If you ever need us, think of us and we shall be there to help you!'

Georgie rode on through the forest till he came to a tall fir tree with a raven's nest in its crown. On the ground below sat two baby ravens, squealing pitifully.

'Our mother and father have flown away and we are all alone! How can we find food for ourselves, poor fledglings that we are, when we can't even fly yet! Oh, help us, please, help us! Find us something to eat, or we shall die of hunger!'

Georgie only hesitated a moment. He jumped off his horse and killed it with his sword, so the young ravens would have ample food.

'Thank you, Georgie,' they cawed happily, 'if you ever need us, think of us and we'll be there to help you!'

Now Georgie had to continue on foot. He walked on for a long time, and when at last he left the forest behind him, he came to a great wide sea. Two fisherman were quarrelling on the shore. They had caught a huge golden fish in their net, and each wanted it for himself.

'The net is mine, so the fish is mine too!' one said.

'What good is your net without my boat and my help!' said the other.

'The next time we catch such a fish, it can be yours!'

'Certainly not! I'll have this one, you can wait for the next!'

'I'll settle your quarrel,' Georgie said. 'Sell the fish to me, I'll pay you handsomely and you can split the money between you.' He pulled out his purse with the money the king had given him for the journey, and handed it over. He did not keep a single coin for himself.

The fishermen were delighted to get such a high price for their catch, and Georgie let the fish go back into the sea. It splashed merrily and dived down, but its head reappeared once more before it swam away. 'Thank you, Georgie, thank you!' the fish cried. 'If you need me, think of me and I'll be there!'

'Where are you going?' the fishermen asked.

'I am searching for Goldie, the golden-haired maiden, but I have no idea where to find her. My master, the old king, wants her for his bride.'

'We can help you,' the fishermen said. 'Goldie is a princess, and she is the daughter of the king who lives in the crystal palace on the island over there. Every morning, as the sun rises, she combs her golden hair, and its glow spreads across the sky and the sea. As you have settled our quarrel, we'll row you across to the island. Be sure you choose the right princess. The king has twelve daughters, but only one with golden hair!'

When Georgie reached the island, he went straight to the king in the crystal palace and asked for his golden-haired daughter as a bride for his own king and master.

'I'll give her to you,' the king agreed, 'but first you must earn the princess. I shall set you three tasks, and you must accomplish one each day. Now rest till tomorrow.'

The next morning the king said to Georgie, 'My daughter had a necklace of precious pearls. The string broke and the pearls have scattered in the long grass in our meadow. Now go and find them, every single one!'

Georgie walked to the meadow, which was very big. He knelt down in the long grass and began to look for the pearls. Though he searched from morning till noon, not one pearl did he find.

'Oh, if only my ants were here, they would help me,' he sighed.

'We are right here to help you!' cried a chorus of tiny voices. And there they all were, swarming round him. 'What do you want?'

'I have to collect the pearls spilled in this meadow, and I can't see a single one!'

'Wait a while, Georgie, and we'll find them all!' cried the ants. True as their word, in a few minutes there was a whole pile of pearls at Georgie's feet. All he had to do was to string them onto the golden

thread. He was about to fasten the thread when a tiny ant came limping towards him. It was lame, for it had lost its leg in the anthill fire.

'Wait, oh please, wait!' the little ant cried. 'Here is another one!'

Georgie took the pearls to the king, and when the king had counted them, not a single one was missing.

'You have done well,' he said. 'Tomorrow I shall set you another task.'

The following morning the king turned to Georgie and said, 'When my daughter Goldie bathed in the sea, she lost a gold ring. Now go and find it.'

Georgie went down to the sea and walked sadly along the shore. Though the water was clear, it was so deep he could not see the sea bed, so what chance had he of ever finding the ring?

'Oh, if only my golden fish were here, it would help me,' he sighed.

There was a sudden flash of light in the sea and the golden fish shot from the depths to the surface. 'I am right here to help you!' it cried. 'What do you want of me?'

'I'm supposed to find a gold ring lost in the sea, and I can't even see the bottom.'

'Why, I swam past a pike wearing a golden ring on its fin only a moment ago! I'll be back with it in a flash!'

In no time at all the golden fish returned, in her mouth the pike with the gold ring on its fin.

Again the king praised Georgie for completing his second task. On the third morning he said, 'If you want me to give you my daughter, Goldie, as a bride for your king, you must bring her the water of life and the water of death. She will need them both.'

Georgie had no idea where to look and he wandered about at random till he came to a deep dark forest.

'Oh, if only my young ravens were here,' he sighed. 'Perhaps they could help me.'

Suddenly, something flew through the air, and there sat the two ravens on a branch above his head. 'We are right here,' they cawed. 'What can we do for you?'

'I've been ordered to fetch the water of death and the water of life, and I don't know where to find them!'

'We know where they are. Be patient a little, we'll be back with them.'

In no time at all the birds returned, each carrying a gourd. One contained the water of life, the other the water of death. Georgie was thrilled with his good fortune and hastened back to the palace.

As he was coming out of the forest, he noticed a spider's web stretched from tree to tree, with a big fat spider sitting in the middle, munching a fly. Georgie took the gourd filled with the water of death and sprinkled a few drops

over the spider, and it fell dead to the ground like an over-ripe cherry. Then he sprinkled the dead fly with the water of life, and soon the fly was wriggling about till it scrambled out of the spider's web and buzzed round Georgie's head joyfully.

'Lucky for you, Georgie, that you revived me,' it buzzed. 'Without

my help you'd never guess which of the twelve princesses is the one you want.'

When the king saw that Georgie had accomplished the third task, he agreed to give him princess Goldie. 'But,' he warned, 'you must pick her out yourself.'

Then he led him into a big hall with a big round table in the centre, and round the table twelve lovely maidens were seated, all exactly alike. Each had her head covered with a long white veil which fell to the ground, so that it was impossible to see whether her hair was dark or fair.

'Here are all my daughters,' said the king. 'Guess which one is Goldie and she shall be yours and you will be able to depart with her at once. If your guess is wrong, you must leave without her.'

Georgie was so afraid, he did not know what to do. Just then, someone whispered in his ear, 'Buzz, buzz! Walk round the table, I'll tell you which one to choose.' It was the fly he had revived with the water of life.

'Not this maiden, not this one, nor this, but . . . this is the one! She is Goldie!'

'Give me this daughter!' Georgie cried, 'She is the one I have earned for my master!'

'You have guessed rightly,' the king agreed. The princess rose from the table, took off her veil, and her golden locks fell in thick waves from head to floor, shining like the morning sun, till they dazzled Georgie's eyes and warmed his heart.

The king gave his daughter a dowry fit for a princess, and Georgie returned with her to his master. The old king's eyes nearly popped out of his head and he jumped for joy when he saw the lovely princess. Straightaway he gave orders for preparations to be made for their wedding.

'I was going to have you hanged for your disobedience,' the king said to Georgie, 'and leave your carcass for the crows. But as you have served me well, I shall only have you beheaded and I shall give you an honourable funeral.'

After Georgie's execution, Goldie begged the old king to give her the body and head of his dead servant. The king could not deny his golden-haired bride anything, and he consented. Goldie placed Georgie's severed head close to his body and sprinkled him with the water of death, and the two grew together at once without leaving even a scar. Then she sprinkled the corpse with the water of life, and Georgie sprang to his feet, as if he were reborn, as lively as a young stag, with youth and health shining in his face.

'Oh, how soundly I have slept,' he cried, rubbing his eyes.

'How true,' Goldie softly agreed, 'you slept soundly indeed. 'And if it were not for me, you would stay asleep till the end of time.'

When the old king saw that Georgie had not only been brought back to life, but that he was younger and more handsome than before, he decided that he, too, would like to grow young and handsome again. At once he gave the order for his head to be cut off and then for his body and head to be sprinkled with the water. So the servants cut off his head and sprinkled him with the water of life; they kept on sprinkling him till they used up all the water, but the head just would not knit with the body. Only then did they try the water of death, and the two grew together at once. But the king was still dead, and he remained dead, for there was no more water of life left to revive him.

As the kingdom could not be left without a king, and as there was no one as wise as Georgie, who understood the language of all animals, he was crowned king, and Goldie queen.

Mr LONG, Mr BROAD AND Mr SHARPEYE

Once upon a time there was an aged king who had an only son. One day he sent for him and said, 'As you know, my dear son, ripe fruit falls off a tree to make room for other fruit to grow. For me, too, the time is almost ripe — it won't be long before the sun will no longer shine upon my old head. But before I die, I would dearly love to see the face of your bride. Get married, my son!'

'How I should like to please you, father!' the prince exclaimed, 'but I have no bride, and I don't know of a maiden whom I wish to marry.'

The old king handed his son a golden key and said, 'Take this key, climb to the top of the tower and from the portraits there select a bride.'

The prince left at once. He had never been up in the tower and he was most curious to see what he would find.

When he reached the very top he saw a small trap door in the ceiling. It was locked, so he opened it with the golden key, raised the flap and climbed up. He found himself in a great hall with a ceiling as dark blue as the sky on a clear night, with silver stars glittering on it. The floor was carpeted in green silk and there were twelve gold-framed, high windows carved in the walls. On the crystal glass of each window was a painting of a beautiful maiden with a crown upon her head, each more beautiful than the last. The prince could hardly bear to tear his eyes away. As he gazed at them in wonder, not knowing which one to choose, the maidens began to move as if they were alive, beckoning him and smiling, but they did not speak.

Then the prince noticed a white curtain drawn across one window. He drew it aside and saw a maiden in a white robe, a silver sash round her waist, a crown of pearls on her head. She was lovelier than all the others, but she looked pale and sad, as if she had risen from her grave.

The prince stood there spellbound, and his heart ached within him. 'She is the only one for me!' he cried, and as he spoke, the maiden bowed her head and blushed like a rose, and all the portraits vanished.

The old king frowned when his son told him of his choice. 'You have chosen unwisely,' he said. 'You have uncovered that which was hidden and your words have thrown you into great danger. That maiden is imprisoned by a wicked wizard in an iron castle. Many have tried to rescue her, but none have returned alive. But what is done, cannot be undone. You have given your word, so go, try your fortune and may you return safe and sound!'

The prince bade his father a fond farewell, mounted his horse and set forth to seek his bride. He rode into a great forest where the path ended and he lost his way. As he was wandering among rocks and thickets, he heard a voice calling to him, 'Hi! Wait!'

The prince turned round and saw a tall, lean fellow trying to catch up with him.

'Take me into your service! You will not regret it!' he said.

'Who are you and what can you do?' the prince asked.

'My name is Mr Long and I can stretch. Do you see the nest in that tall pine tree? I'll fetch it for you without even having to climb.' With that, this strange fellow began to stretch; he grew and grew till he was as tall as the pine. He picked up the nest, swiftly shrank to his normal size and handed the nest to the prince.

'You certainly live up to your name,' said the prince. 'But what use are birds' nests to me if you can't lead me out of this forest?'

'Easily done!' Mr Long remarked and once again he stretched himself till he was three times as tall as the highest tree in the forest. He had a good look round, then said, 'I'll take you the shortest way out of this forest.' Mr Long shrank again, took the horse's reins and soon they had left the forest behind.

An endless plain now lay before them, and beyond it rose high grey rocks like ramparts of a great city, and beyond the rocks stretched a range of mountains covered with forests.

'Look, master, here comes my friend,' Mr Long cried, pointing across the plain. 'You should hire him too, he would be very useful.'

'Call him over here then, so I can have a look at him.'

'He is too far away to hear me,' said Mr Long, 'I'll nip over and fetch him.'

Mr Long stretched himself till his head scraped the clouds, took two or three strides, put his friend on his shoulder and was back again. The prince found himself looking at a fat little fellow, as round as a barrel.

'Who are you and what can you do?' asked the prince.

'My name is Mr Broad and I can expand,' the stranger replied and, to demonstrate, he began to swell. 'But you'd better get out of my way, master, and fast!'

At first, the prince did not understand why he should move, but when he saw Mr Long running for the forest, he followed at a gallop. It was high time too, for Mr Broad would have surely crushed him, horse and all, so quickly did his tummy expand in all directions; he looked like a giant balloon. At last, he stopped blowing himself up, and blew the air out of his tummy instead, and it came out with such force that the forest swayed. And he was his normal size again.

'You made me run for my life!' said the prince. 'But one doesn't find a fellow like you every day. Come with me.'

The trio travelled on till they came to the rocks, and there they met a man with a scarf over his eyes.

'This is another friend of mine,' said Mr Long. 'You should employ him, too. He will more than pay for his keep.'

'Who are you?' asked the prince, 'and why are your eyes bandaged? Surely you cannot see the way?'

'Oh, yes I can, master! I have to keep my eyes covered because I see too well! I see as much with my bandaged eyes as another with his unbound. When I take off my scarf, I can see right through everything, and when I look sharply at any object, it either bursts into flame or shatters to pieces. This is why they call me Mr Sharpeye.'

To demonstrate what he could do, he turned to the rock opposite, took off his scarf and stared at it. Straightaway the rock began to crumble, with fragments flying in all directions till it was but a heap of sand. Something in the pile of sand glittered like fire. Mr Sharpeye picked it up and gave it to the prince. It was pure gold.

'You're an invaluable fellow!' exclaimed the prince. 'I would be a fool not to take advantage of your services! But as your sight is so good, please look and see how far it is to the iron castle, and what is happening inside it.'

Mr Sharpeye gazed into the distance and said, 'If you were travelling on your own, master, it would take you a year or more to reach

it, but with our help you'll get there this very night. In fact a supper is being prepared for us right now!'

'And what is my bride doing?'

Mr Sharpeye looked again, then chanted,

> 'The tower is high, the bars are strong
> She weeps, she sighs, she waits so long,
> The princess who must captive dwell,
> Under the wicked wizard's spell.'

'Good fellows,' cried the prince, 'help me free her!'

They all promised to do just that, and with their aid all obstacles were conquered. Mr Long stepped across plains and over mountains, Mr Broad drank up lakes, Mr Sharpeye burned paths through the grey rocks. As the sun started to slide to the west, the mountains became lower and less forbidding, the forests thinned and the rocks hid amongst the heather. As the sun dropped nearer to the horizon, the iron castle appeared before them. Just as the sun was finally vanishing from sight, they crossed the drawbridge, which rose swiftly behind them with a thunderous noise.

The prince put his horse in the stable, where everything had been prepared, and then they all entered the castle. In the courtyard, stable and halls they found many richly dressed noblemen and servants, but not one of them moved - they had all been turned to stone. The prince and his friends walked through several fine chambers, till they came to a great dining room. It was ablaze with lights and had a large table set for four people in the centre, with many delicacies and drinks spread upon it. They waited and waited, expecting someone to come. Nobody did, and as they were hungry, they sat down and ate and drank to their hearts' content.

Suddenly the door flew open and the wizard entered. He was a bent old man with a bald head and a grey, flowing beard. His long black robe was fastened at the waist by three iron hoops. He was holding the hand of the most beautiful maiden dressed in white; a silver sash circled her waist and a crown of pearls adorned her head, but she was pale and mournful as if she had risen from her grave.

The prince recognized her at once and rose to meet her, but before he could say a word, the wizard spoke. 'I know why you are here! You want to take this princess away from me. So be it, you can have her, providing you guard her so well these next three nights that I shall not be able to steal her from you. If you fail, you will all be turned to stone, as all those who have come before you.'

83

The wizard led the princess to a chair and disappeared. The prince could not take his eyes off the lovely maiden. He spoke to her, asking her all sorts of things, but she did not reply, or smile, but remained silent and still as if carved in marble. The prince sat at her side, determined not to close an eye that night so she should not slip away from him. Just to make doubly sure, his friend Mr Long stretched and wound himself like a rope round the room's walls; Mr Broad blotted the doorway by puffing himself out so that not even a mouse could squeeze past; and Mr Sharpeye stood guard in the centre of the room. But they began to doze and soon they were asleep.

The prince awoke just before dawn and, when he realised the princess was gone, he felt as if someone had plunged a knife into his very heart.

'Whatever can I do?' he cried, waking his servants.

'Do not worry, sir,' said Mr Sharpeye, gazing intently out of the window. 'I can see her! A hundred miles from here lies a deep forest. In the middle of the forest there is an oak tree, and on the very top of the tree is an acorn — and that acorn is our princess. If I sit on Mr Long's shoulder, I'll reach her in no time at all.'

Mr Long sat Mr Sharpeye on his shoulder, stretched himself and strode out, ten miles at a stride, with Sharpeye pointing the way. They returned as quick as lightning and, the moment the prince dropped the acorn on to the floor, it turned into the princess.

The sun was just rising as the wizard burst into the room, smiling with malice. When he saw the princess, his brow knitted in anger. He growled and — bang! One of the iron hoops round his waist snapped and crashed to the floor. He seized the princess and led her away.

All that day the prince had nothing to do but wander through the rooms and courtyards of the castle and marvel at the strange things he found. All around him it seemed as if all life had been severed in one swift moment. In one room he saw a nobleman, his sword raised, ready to strike, as if he were about to cut his foe in half, but he had been turned to stone before he could deliver the blow. In another room was a knight who had just tripped over the threshold, but had been struck motionless by the wizard before he fell to the floor. By the chimney breast of the kitchen sat a servant, a chunk of meat in one hand and just about to stuff a piece into his mouth with the other; but his hand never reached his mouth, for he had been turned to stone as he raised it. There were many other motionless figures caught in the middle of whatever they had been doing by the wizard's evil spell. Even the horses did not escape, for they, too, had been turned to stone. Within and around the castle everything was dead and desolate: the trees were leafless, the meadows brown and withered; the river did not flow; there was not a single bird to be heard, not a single flower to be seen, not a single little fish darting through the water.

During the day the prince and his companions were fed royally; the food carried itself in and the wine poured itself out. After supper that night, the doors burst open again and the wizard brought in the princess for the prince to guard. They were all determined to keep awake, but try as they might, they fell asleep as before.

When the prince awoke just before dawn and saw that the princess was gone, he leapt to his feet and shook Mr Sharpeye by the shoulder. 'Up with you, Mr Sharpeye, and be sharp about it! Can you see the princess?'

Mr Sharpeye rubbed his eyes and cried, 'Yes, I see her! Two hundred miles from here is a mountain. In the mountain is a rock and in the rock itself is a jewel. She is that jewel. If Mr Long takes me, we will bring her back.'

Mr Long stretched himself out into the clouds and, with Mr Sharpeye on his shoulder, he strode out, each step twenty miles. When Mr Sharpeye turned his piercing eyes upon the mountain, it turned to dust, and amongst the dust glittered the jewel. They brought it back to the prince, who dropped it on the floor just in time, for the wizard burst into the room as the jewel turned into the princess. When the wizard saw her, his eyes flashed with rage, and crash! The second iron hoop broke and thundered to the floor. The wizard growled angrily and led the princess away.

The day passed as the day before, and after supper the wizard brought in the princess for the last time. He gave the prince a mocking glance and said scornfully, 'Tonight we shall see who is the better man. Whether you will win, or I!'

The prince and his friends tried harder than ever to keep awake; they did not even sit down, but walked up and down all night long. But try as they might they fell asleep as they walked, and the princess slipped away.

When the prince awoke the following morning, he shook Mr Sharpeye hard and cried, 'On your feet, Sharpeye, look for the princess!'

'This time, master, she is far, far away,' said Mr Sharpeye, after staring into the distance for a long time. 'Three hundred miles from here is the Black Sea and, in the middle of the sea, at the very bottom, lies a shell holding a gold ring. The princess is that ring. But never fear. Let me take Mr Broad with me today, for I shall need his help.'

Mr Long sat Mr Sharpeye on one shoulder and Mr Broad on the other, and strode out, each step thirty miles. When they came to the Black Sea, though Mr Long stretched his arm as far as it would go, he could not reach the bottom.

'Wait! This is where I come in,' Mr Broad cried, and he blew him-

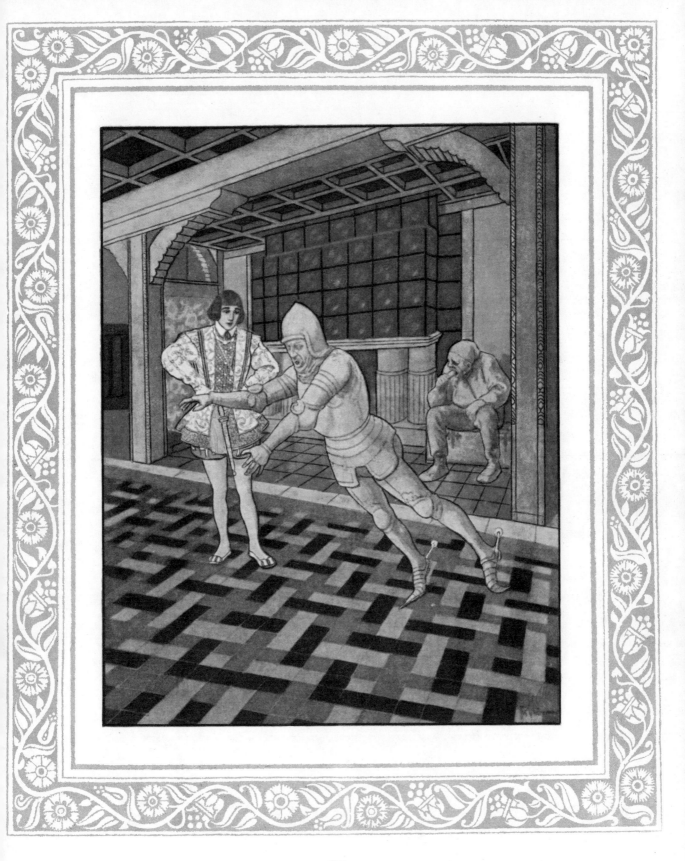

self out as much as he could. Then he took a deep breath and began to drink up the ocean. Soon the sea was so shallow that Mr Long was easily able to pick up the shell and take out the gold ring.

On their way back Mr Long found it difficult to hurry, as he was carrying Mr Broad with half the sea inside him, and so he dropped Mr Broad in a wide valley. He bounced as he landed and the water gushed out of his mouth with such force that in a minute the valley turned into a huge lake. Mr Broad himself only managed to crawl out in the nick of time.

Meanwhile, back in the castle, the prince was anxiously waiting. The sun was already rising and there was no sign of his servants. The brighter the rays of the sun became, the more troubled he grew. Cold sweat broke out on his brow. Then the sun appeared in the east like a fine ribbon of fire and, at that moment, the door burst open and the wizard stood on the threshold. When he saw the empty room, he roared victoriously and walked in. Just then, there was a sound of splintering glass as the gold ring smashed through the window and fell at their feet, and suddenly the princess stood there before them.

Mr Sharpeye had seen what was going on in the castle and knew that the prince was in great danger. So Mr Long leapt forward and flung the ring into the room from a distance. The wizard cursed and raged till the castle shook and the last iron hoop burst open. With that the wizard turned into a black crow and flew away through the shattered window.

At once the lovely princess was able to speak. Blushing like a rose, she thanked the prince for setting her free. The whole castle came to life again. The knight in the hall who had drawn his sword swished it through the air and then put it away; the man who had tripped over the threshold fell down, but jumped up at once, rubbing his nose to make sure it was still there; the servant sitting by the chimney breast

stuffed the piece of meat into his mouth and munched away; everyone carried on doing what they had been doing before being turned to stone. The horses in the stables stamped and neighed joyously; the trees were covered in leaves, the meadows were bright with colourful flowers, the lark sang sweetly overhead and a school of tiny fish swam to and fro in the fast flowing river. Everything was alive, everyone was happy and gay!

Many lords and gentlemen gathered in the hall where the prince stood, to thank him for setting them free. But he brushed their thanks aside and said, 'If it were not for my companions, Mr Long, Mr Broad and Mr Sharpeye, I too would have been turned to stone.'

He set out straightaway for his father's palace with his bride, and Mr Long and Mr Sharpeye. All the noblemen came with them and on the way, they met Mr Broad and he came too.

The old king wept for joy at his son's success, for he had feared that the prince would never return. Soon a merry wedding was held, which went on for three weeks and all the lords and gentlemen whom the prince had set free were guests.

After the wedding, the prince begged Mr Long, Mr Broad and Mr Sharpeye to stay with him for good, but they refused, though he said they would never need to work again.

An idle life was not to their taste, and they were soon off. They are probably still wandering about the world now, helping people when they can.

KING POLECAT

Long ago there was a time when in Bohemia every chicken community was self ruling. It had its own yard and its own refuse tip where the birds could scrape and peck away to their hearts' content, under the watchful eye of the master cockerel. Anything the hens dug out they would keep, but when the cockerel unearthed a tasty grain, he often presented it to his favourite chic, or he gobbled it up himself. If some hen happened to object, a sharp nip with his beak soon put an end to her complaints. It only needed the master cockerel to 'cock-a-doodle-doo' just once, and all the roosters in the village joined in. And so they all lived for ages and ages, respectful, obedient and in perfect harmony.

But, alas, one day the frogs grew tired of the old system and they croaked and they croaked till they croaked a long legged stork into becoming their king. Seeing this, the cockerels and hens did not wish to be left behind the old frogs, and so they decided they would have to have their own king, too.

They held a council meeting and started debating what they should do and how they should do it. They were all of one mind until it came to the choice of a king, for then they started to bicker and peck at one another.

Nobody wanted someone else ruling them, they all wanted to be the ruler. All the cockerels were spoiling for a fight and they went for each other, till feathers flew everywhere.

In order to stop all the bickering and fighting, an old wise rooster suggested that they should choose a foreign king and straightaway he said that Mr Polecat would be highly suitable, for apart from having a good set of fangs he was strong enough and big enough to put the fear of God into one and all. Surely a chap like him would be able to keep law and order amongst them? Everyone was in favour and so Mr Polecat was sent for, to be offered a proper contract.

Mr Polecat listened to their request and he seemed so kind and so gracious, promising to honour all their old rights and freedoms. He assured one and all that he would protect the fowl population against the birds of prey who carried away their chicks, and against the marten, who snatched their eggs; even against the thieving sparrows who stole the grain right in front of their very beaks. Mr Polecat also promised that he would make the biggest and the handsomest cockerels his royal councillors, attendants and officers.

The hens and the cockerels liked what they heard and they put Mr Polecat on the royal throne with great fanfare and ceremony. They were all terribly pleased to have such a powerful and kind king.

Before very long, King Polecat hankered after chicken blood. He decided that the best way to get some would be to find one of his subjects guilty of something or other, so he would have the excuse to bite off his head. He certainly had no intention of publicly showing his true polecat character and scaring off the rest of his subjects.

He summoned a nice fat rooster and said, 'What can you smell?'

The cockerel who was a truly honest soul replied, 'Begging Your Majesty's pardon, there is a terrible smell here.'

That terrible smell was, of course, the foul smell every polecat emits, even when sitting on the royal chicken throne!

'You rude, brazen villain!' the polecat cried. 'How dare you talk like this to your king and master?' And snap! He bit off the rooster's head.

Then, he summoned a second cockerel and asked the same question. The cockerel could see the headless body of his friend and he noticed, too, that His Majesty's mouth was smudged with blood. The cockerel realized that he was up to his neck in trouble and began to tremble with fear from head to foot. He was trembling so hard, he could not utter a single word.

'Why are you shaking?' roared the king. 'I suspect you have a bad conscience. Tell me what you can smell!'

The cockerel summoned all his strength, bowed and clucked in a thin voice. 'Your Royal Highness, I smell the most heavenly perfume.'

'Shame on you, you old liar!' cried the king. 'Your flattery will get you nowhere!' And snap! He bit off his head, too.

By now, the polecat had had enough but he was enjoying the game so much that he called yet another cockerel and asked him what he could smell.

This old rooster was a crafty fellow. Though he was well aware of both the headless bodies and of the blood marks on the royal whiskers, he pretended he had not seen them.

He bowed several times to the king and replied, 'Begging your pardon, Your Royal Majesty, but this wet weather has given me the most dreadful cold and I cannot smell a thing!'

The king realised that the cockerel had escaped the trap he had set for him and, because no other ideas came into his polecat head, he could only smile graciously and allow the cockerel to depart.

THE THREE SPINNERS

There was a poor widow who had an only daughter called Lizzie. They owned no field, not even a cow — all they had in the world was a spinning wheel, and so they made their living by spinning. Though Lizzie was pretty and well-behaved, she was borne idle. Just the mention of the spinning wheel sent her into a flood of tears and, if her mother forced her to spin, the results left a lot to be desired.

One day the mother's patience ran out. She lost her temper and slapped her daughter. This sent Lizzie into such hysterics that you could hear her for miles around.

The queen happened to be riding by and, when she heard the heartrending sobbing and moaning, she stopped and entered the little cottage, convinced that a great calamity must have happened inside.

When she saw Lizzie weeping so pitifully, she asked, 'What is the matter, dear child?'

'My mother has been hitting me!' the maiden cried.

'Why did you hit this poor child?' asked the queen, turning to the widow.

The mother did not know what to reply, for she was ashamed to confess to the queen that Lizzie was so very lazy. So she said, 'I have quite a problem with this daughter of mine, Your Majesty, for she never wants to leave the spinning wheel alone. If she had her way, she would sit by the wheel day and night. I am afraid I got angry with her today and slapped her. This is why she cries.'

The queen took an instant liking to the girl, for spinning was a great hobby of hers, too. 'I have a suggestion to make,' she said to the widow. 'As your daughter so loves to spin, let me have her. I shall look after her well. I have some fine flax in my palace. If she works as hard there as she has at home, she will do well.'

The mother was thrilled with this idea and before long, she was bidding the queen and Lizzie goodbye.

When they reached the palace, the queen took Lizzie by the hand and led her to three rooms which were filled from floor to ceiling with flax. It was of the finest quality, sparkling like silver and gold and as soft as unspun silk.

'Work hard, lovely maiden,' the queen then said. 'If you turn all this flax to thread, I will give you my son for a husband. When he marries he will become king and you shall be queen.'

A magnificent spinning wheel was brought in for Lizzie, made of ebony and gold. There was a huge basket too, filled with empty cane spools. Lizzie was left all alone and she sat by the window and wept.

She knew that even if she were to spin day after day from morn till night for a hundred years, she could not work through such a mountain of flax. 'I hate spinning anyway,' she moaned, 'so what chance have I?' So she just sat there, bathed in tears, right through the night and through the next morning, without even lifting her little finger.

The queen came at noon to see how Lizzie was progressing with her work and she was most surprised that the girl had not touched the spinning wheel. 'I missed my mother so much, I just cried and cried,' Lizzie lied, 'and I was too upset to work.'

The queen believed her, and said to comfort the girl, 'Don't be homesick any more, Lizzie, and work that much harder tomorrow, so that you will win my son!

Alone again, Lizzie went over to the window and stared out, sighing and doing nothing that day nor the following morning.

At noon, the queen returned and she was shocked to see that again no work had been done. This time Lizzie had another excuse ready. 'So much weeping left me with a terrible headache,' she lied. 'I just couldn't do a thing!'

The queen seemed satisfied with this explanation but as she was leaving, she warned, 'It is high time, Lizzie, for you to set to work if you want to win my son and be a queen!'

Yet, the next time the queen came at noon, everything was as before. Lazy Lizzie had not lifted a finger.

The queen grew angry and cried, 'I shall not listen to any more excuses! If you don't make a start today, not only will my son never be yours, but you shall be locked in a dark tower with only frogs, snakes and scorpions for company and I shall leave you there to perish of hunger! Then you won't be able to cheat me or be lazy ever again.'

Stamping her feet crossly, the queen slammed the door behind her.

Now Lizzie really had something to worry about! Just the thought of the next day brought her out in a cold sweat. What was she to do? Threading the distaff, she sat at the spinning wheel and began to spin. Yet, how could she go on spinning when she was so very, very lazy? So Lizzie let the spinning wheel be and, standing by the window, she wept over her fate and wrung her hands in despair.

It was almost dark, when there was a knock on the window. When Lizzie peered out, she saw three ugly old hags standing there. The first had a lower lip which was so stretched it hung right over her chin. The second had a thumb on her right hand as wide as the palm of her hand, and the right foot of the third was so long and flattened, it looked as if it had been run over by a cart.

The sight of the old hags made Lizzie jump with fright, but they smiled kindly and beckoned her to open the window and not be afraid.

'Good evening, lovely maiden,' they said. 'Why are you weeping so?'

Lizzie took heart and she sobbed, 'Oh, how could I be anything but sad and brokenhearted, when I've been told to spin all the flax you can see here and in two other rooms just like this one!' And she told the three old women everything. 'It is no use,' she ended, 'for if I work till my dying day, I'll never finish!'

The old women smiled and one of them said, 'If you promise to invite us to your wedding and to seat us next to you at your table, and if you won't be ashamed of us in front of your guests, we shall spin all this flax in no time at all.'

Lizzie couldn't believe her ears. 'I'll do anything you ask,' she cried, 'but please make a start now!'

With that, the three old women climbed in, told Lizzie to go to sleep, and then they set to work. The one with the broad thumb pulled the fibre, the one with the long lower lip licked and smoothed it and the third with the flat foot worked the treadle and the wheel; the three made a very good team.

When Lizzie woke up the following morning, she saw to her joy a lovely big pile of spools with the finest yarn. There was a great big gap in the flax mountain, large enough for her to hide in! The old women bade her goodbye, promising to return at dusk, and out of the window they hopped.

When at noon the queen saw the huge pile of beautiful yarn, she was very pleasantly surprised and she praised Lizzie for having worked so hard.

That same evening the three old women knocked on the window

again and Lizzie gladly let them in. And so it continued, night after night. They came at dusk and departed with the dawn, and whilst Lizzie slept soundly, the flax mountain shrank and shrank till the first room was quite empty.

The queen marvelled each day at the perfection of the yarn and at Lizzie's diligence. So often she remarked, 'Oh, my dear child, how I have wronged you!'

By the time the second room had been almost cleared, the queen started the wedding preparations.

When the third room was nearly empty of flax, Lizzie thanked the old women most sincerely for their help. 'Just don't forget your promise,' they reminded her. 'You shall not regret it.'

When the last traces of flax had disappeared, everything for the wedding was ready, and the young prince was very thrilled with his beautiful, hardworking young bride. 'Your wish is my command,' he said to her.

Remembering the three kind old women, Lizzie said, 'I have three old aunts at home. They are very poor and simple, but they have been very good to me. May I ask them to our wedding?'

The young prince and his mother, the old queen, gladly agreed.

On the wedding day, just as the guests were about to be seated for the feast, the doors burst open and the three ugly old women rushed in, dressed in ridiculous and old-fashioned clothes.

The minute the bride saw them, she ran to greet them. 'Welcome, dearest aunts, welcome! Come and sit down here, by my side!'

The guests looked at each other, stifling their laughter. They did not dare laugh aloud, for fear of angering their new king and his bride. He and his mother, the old queen, turned as red as beetroots, but they had given their permission for the aunts to come, so they could not object now.

Lizzie helped the old women to the best foods and wines. 'Eat and drink to your hearts' content, my dearest aunts,' she said. 'Let me re-pay your kindness a little.'

After the feast, as the guests were leaving the tables, the young king approached the first old woman and said, 'Tell me, dear aunt, what has made your right foot so long and flat?'

'Too much spinning, young man.'

The young king then went to the second old woman, the one with the thumb as wide as the palm of her hand. 'Tell me, dear aunt,' he asked, 'what has made your thumb so wide?'

'Too much spinning, young man.'

The young king then turned to the third old woman. 'Tell me, dear aunt, what has made your lower lip so long that it hangs over your chin?'

'Too much spinning, young man.'

The king, alarmed at their words, hastened to his bride and said, 'I command you that to your dying day you will never again touch the spinning wheel. Now promise you will obey! I could not bear you to end up with such a flattened long foot, or a thumb as wide as your palm, or an ugly lower lip hanging over your chin!'

As he spoke, the three old women disappeared, no one knew where. But they were often in Lizzie's thoughts, and she blessed them for helping her. She remained faithful and true to her hus-band's command. Never did she keep a promise so gladly!

THE MISCHIEVOUS DEMONS
I

Once there was a farmer called Old Man Thistle. When he was going to the market one day, he found a lone black chicken under a pear tree, in a field. The poor wee thing was all soaked through and trembling with cold and cheeping forlornly. Old Man Thistle put it under his coat and when he got home, he left it behind the oven to dry out. Afterwards he let the bird out in the yard with his other hens.

During that night, when everyone was asleep, he heard a rustling sound in the larder, followed by a creaky voice, part human, part chicken, 'Come and see, old chap, I've brought you some spuds!'

Old Man Thistle leapt from his bed and ran to the larder, and what did he find there? Three piles of potatoes and a fiery chicken flying from one pile to the other!

'Where did you get these from?' said Old Man Thistle.

'Don't you know?' cackled the chicken. 'I'm a demon from hell and I'm here to stay!'

'Away with you, you mischievous creature!' the farmer cried, and spat in disgust. He slammed the door and marched back to bed, too worried to go back to sleep, for now he knew what he had brought into his household. At daybreak, as soon as he could see, he threw all the potatoes on to the manure heap.

The next night he heard again, 'Come on, old chap, I've brought you wheat, rye and barley!'

This time Old Man Thistle did not bother to check, but he was trembling like a leaf and praying, repeating all the time, 'Deliver us from evil!' At daybreak, as soon as it was light, armed with a spade and a broom he swept and shovelled out all the corn to the very last grain.

Oh, how miserable he was! Old Man Thistle was at his wits end, and terribly anxious that none of the neighbours would notice what was going on. But notice they did. They saw in the dead of night a flying fiery object landing in the Thistle household, yet it did not set anything alight. And during the day, the woman next-door saw the strange black chicken in the yard. At once a rumour started that Old Man Thistle had made a pact with the devil. Some people refused to listen to such accusations, for they knew that Old Man Thistle was an honest man, so they decided to give him a word of warning.

They went to visit him and he told them exactly what had happened. 'What shall I do?' he asked.

'There is only one thing for it,' a young farmer replied. 'You must kill that little monster!' With that he seized a stick and threw it at the black chicken. The chicken ducked, flew on to his back and started attacking him, biting, pecking and screeching with every blow.

'I am a demon, a demon, a demon!'

Now, everyone advised Old Man Thistle to sell up and move away, for the demon would surely remain in the building. Old Man Thistle grasped at this hope and looked for a buyer, but no one was prepared to buy a farm with such a devilish sitting tenant.

But Old Man Thistle was determined to rid himself of that little devil at all costs. So he sold his corn and all his cattle, leaving himself only the essential items. Then he bought another building in a neighbouring village and started to move. When he had loaded his cart, he walked over to his old thatched home and set it alight. It stood on its own, so he could do no damage to the property of others.

As his whip cracked through the air and he was setting off, he took one last look at the burning house and muttered, 'Burn to death, you little monster! At least I'll get something for the land.'

'Hi, hi, hi!' A sound behind him made Old Man Thistle freeze. He looked around, and there was the black chicken, perched on an old tub, waving its wings and singing,

'I'm glad to shout, we're moving out,
We're on our way, and from today
Elsewhere I'll steal, for our next meal!'

Old Man Thistle was stunned. 'What am I to do?' he groaned. Then he thought that maybe the creature could be persuaded to leave, if he fed it royally. So he instructed his wife to give the demon a regular dish of the best milk and three cream buns to go with it. The demon enjoyed them, but he didn't look as if he intended to move.

One day at dusk, their farmhand returned from the fields and saw

the cream buns on the stairs, placed there for the demon. He was so hungry he gobbled them up. 'Why should they be wasted on that child of the devil?' he muttered to himself.

But in a trice, the chicken was on his back, pecking him and screeching, 'This for the first bun - this for the second - and this for the third!'

The farmhand was black and blue for days. In fact, he was in such a state, that he could not move at all the next morning.

When Old Man Thistle found his labourer in such a bad way, he begged the little demon to move away, for no one would be prepared to work on the farm otherwise.

'Ha, ha, ha,' the black chicken clucked, and sang,

'Put me where you found me,
That's all you have to do.
Take me to the pear tree,
And so, goodbye to you!'

Old Man Thistle grabbed the chicken and ran to the pear tree. He put the bird down and was never bothered by the demon again.

II

I know a tale about a farmer's wife in another village who housed a little demon, a goblin this time. Listen how she came to him.

A stranger came one day trying to sell an old rifle to the farmer. The farmer didn't want to buy. 'What would I do with it?' he asked. 'I haven't the cash to spare.'

'All I want for it are three pennies,' the stranger went on. (Apparently a goblin never sells for anything but three pennies).

'Well, if that is all you want, I'll keep the rifle,' the farmer agreed. 'I'll even give you a bit more.'

The stranger wouldn't take a penny extra. He handed the rifle to the farmer, who hung it on a nail in the wall.

During the night the rifle disappeared, but a goblin turned up in the yard. Most of the time he stayed hidden on top of the stove and no one ever saw him, except the farmer's wife and a kitchen maid.

Now, a very strange thing happened after the goblin joined the household. The cows gave a lot more milk and were never sick. Because of this the farmer's wife took a liking to the goblin and each day she gave him a full dish of cream.

The goblin was enjoying himself and getting up to all sorts of mischief.

One day, the kitchen maid was sitting on a bench mashing potatoes. The goblin squatted beside her and whenever the girl's glance strayed, in went his greedy fingers and out came a handful of potatoes straight into his mouth!

When the kitchen maid caught him at it, she hit him with the masher. 'Away with you, you little rogue!' she cried. 'Keep your claws out of my pan!'

The goblin swore he would have his revenge.

That morning, the mistress had bought the maid a brand new pair of shoes, and the girl had left them on a stool. The goblin snatched the shoes and tore them to smithereens. The maid burst into tears, and ran wailing to her mistress. The farmer's wife rushed to the scene - she looked - and she looked - but the shoes were whole again as if nothing had ever happened to them.

The farmhands and the dairy maids couldn't move an inch without the goblin's knowledge and he always told on them. Whenever someone pinched a bit of butter, or slipped a bread roll or two into his pocket, or when the dairy maid, while milking the cows, filled a jug for herself, the mistress was informed at once, and they were all in trouble.

No wonder then that the workers spread malicious gossip about their mistress keeping a demon in her household. It soon became common knowledge.

The farmer's wife hated to be the talk of the village, and she regretfully decided that the only way to put an end to it was to get rid of the goblin. She didn't know how, till someone suggested she should ask the same stranger who sold her the demon to make him go away again. The man arrived and he sprinkled flour all over the building and the yard. Then he began to recite a magic formula to exorcise the demon and drive him out.

The goblin shrieked to high heaven, he didn't want to go, but he had no choice. He left a trail of footprints similar to dog's paws, right across the kitchen, through the hall and up the stairs, up to the tiny open window in the attic.

The farmer's wife never saw the goblin again.

III

I heard of another case about a demon on a sheep farm. They say he was an elf, for he was just like a little boy, except that he had claws on his hands and feet. Many amusing tales are known about him. He loved to tease dogs and cats, and no one could have called him the farm workers' best friend, for he never missed anything that was going on, and never kept it to himself. No wonder the whole bunch of them had not a good word to say about the elf, but they were afraid to do him harm, fearing his revenge. In any case, the sheep farmer would not have listened to their complaints, probably because since the little demon moved in, illnesses among the sheep moved out.

During the winter, the elf spent most of his time above the stove, keeping himself warm. Whenever the servant girl brought husks into the kitchen to scald, he always jumped into the tub, shouting, 'Hop and plonk on to the husks!'

One day, she played a nasty trick on him. She came in with the tub as usual, but she had filled it outside with boiling water and just scattered a few husks on top.

'Hop and plonk on to the husks!' the elf cried, and plonk! In he went too. My word, did he jump out again, like a shot, and screaming and writhing with pain. And the servant girl just stood there, roaring with laughter, gloating over his agony.

The elf, of course, didn't let this pass. When the maid was climbing a ladder, he entangled her body, arms and legs into it in such a way that she was well and truly stuck, and it took hours and hours to untangle her again.

During the summer, the farm labourers slept in the hayloft. One night the elf followed and sat himself halfway up the ladder. He started to tease the dogs sleeping by the barn in the yard. First he tickled them with one foot, then with the other, chanting,

'This foot, that foot
Which one will you grab?'

The dogs were going berserk, and the farmhands above were angry that their sleep was being disturbed. One man got up, picked up a bundle of hay and threw it on top of the elf, who went crashing to the ground, hay and all. The dogs greeted him in a most unkindly manner and he only just managed to escape their sharp teeth.

The farmhand knew the elf would be after him, so he watched his step and gave the little demon a wide berth; but he did not escape. When he was with the sheep in the meadow one day, he sat down to rest in front of a haystack. He heard a sudden rustling noise above and, before he knew what was what, the whole lot came crashing down on to his head. He screamed and he screamed and the farmhands gathered round him, but try as they might, they couldn't get the hay out of his hair, so expertly had it been knotted in.

There was nothing else for it - he had to have the lot shaved off! And the next time he took the sheep to pasture, and passed under a wild pear tree, there was the elf, sitting in its crown, munching a carrot and chanting mockingly, 'Hi, there baldy! Where's your hair?'

THE BLACKSMITH'S THREE WISHES

It happened very long ago when Christ and Saint Peter were wandering about the world. One evening they found themselves at a blacksmith's forge and they asked for a bed for the night. The blacksmith greeted them warmly, tossed his hammer aside and made them most welcome.

After a good supper he said to his guests, 'I can see you are both tired out from your long journey and badly in need of a good night's rest. And what a hot, humid day it has been, too. Have my bed and sleep soundly. I'll put my head down on the straw in the barn.' With that the blacksmith bade them goodnight and went away. When morning came, he served his guests breakfast and accompanied them part of the way. In parting, he said, 'I gave what I had. There is no need for you to thank me.'

Saint Peter tugged Christ by the sleeve and whispered in his ear, 'Master, will you not reward this man for his good heart and warm welcome?'

'A reward on this earth is a worthless one,' Christ replied. 'I shall prepare his reward in heaven!' But he turned to the blacksmith and said, 'Ask whatever you want, I shall grant you three wishes.'

This pleased the blacksmith greatly. He thought a little, then said, 'In that case, my Lord, let me live another hundred years in good health as I am today.'

'It shall be done,' Christ answered. 'What is your second wish?'

The blacksmith thought again. 'What should I ask? I do very well on this earth. I earn all I need by my trade. Grant me then that I'll have plenty of work for the rest of my days.'

'It shall be done,' Christ replied. 'Now tell me, what is your last wish?'

The blacksmith at first could not think of anything else, but then he said, 'As you are so kind, my Lord, then make anyone who sits on the chair you used in my forge stick fast to it, till I give him leave to go!'

Saint Peter thought this a very funny request, but Christ agreed. 'It shall be done,' he said.

Christ and Saint Peter then travelled on and the blacksmith happily hurried home.

Everything that Christ had promised came true. All his friends and neighbours eventually died, but the blacksmith still enjoyed the best of health; he had plenty of work, too, and he sang all day long.

But all good things come to an end. One day, the hundred years were up and Death knocked on his door.

'It is I, Death. I have come for you!'

'Welcome to my forge! What a distinguished visitor!', the blacksmith cried, a crafty smile on his face. 'Come in, sir, do come in! Just let me put away my tools tidily in their place, I shan't be long. Why don't you sit down in this chair? Travelling all round the world the way you do must be truly exhausting!'

The unsuspecting Death sat down and the blacksmith burst into laughter. 'Now here you'll sit and here you'll stay till I give the word!'

Death struggled to rise, his bones rattling, his sparse teeth grinding with rage; but it was no use, he was well and truly stuck, as if someone had nailed him to the chair.

The blacksmith laughed and laughed till he thought he would split his sides; he slammed the door shut and went about his business, pleased that he need not fear Death again now that he had him trapped at home.

But his joy did not last long. He soon discovered he had made a mistake.

He had a nice fat pig in the sty and to celebrate, he decided to slaughter it and to smoke it, for he was very fond of ham and bacon. So he took his axe and gave the pig such a blow to its head, he knocked it right over. But as he reached for his knife to slit its throat and drain its blood to make his favourite black puddings, the pig suddenly rose to its feet, snorting and grunting, and before the blacksmith recovered from the shock, it had run away.

'Wait till I catch you, you beast!' the blacksmith cried. He then went to a shed and pulled out a goose which he had been fattening up for the past two weeks. 'I'll feast on you instead,' he said, 'seeing my black puddings and my ham have run away!' He took his knife and slit the goose's throat but, to his astonishment, not a drop of blood fell from the wound and the moment he pulled out his knife, the wound healed! As he stood there, stunned and bewildered, the goose slipped out of his hands, cackling shrilly, and fled after the pig.

All this was too much for the blacksmith. He had been so pleased with himself that day, and now he couldn't even celebrate with a good roast. He decided to let the goose and the pig be, and he went over to the dovecot for a pair of pigeons. To prevent them from playing the same trick, he laid them side by side on the chopping block and, with one swift blow of his axe, he chopped off both their heads.

'You'll do for now,' he grunted, throwing the headless bodies to the ground. But wonder of wonders! The moment they touched the ground, the heads knitted with the necks and, screeching loudly, the pigeons flew away.

The truth suddenly dawned on the blacksmith, and he struck his forehead with his fist. 'What a fool I am,' he cried. 'I never thought of this. Of course, nothing can die when Death is my prisoner!'

The idea of never tasting a nice slice of ham, or his favourite black pudding, or a succulent goose, or a pair of roast pigeons did not please him at all. But what was he to do? Set Death free? Oh, no, not that! The first thing Death would do would be to wring his own neck. The blacksmith therefore decided to live on pease pudding and porridge, and to bake buns in the oven instead of roasting meat. 'After all, they'll taste good too!' he consoled himself.

The blacksmith lived this way for quite some time, till his supplies ran out. By the following spring, there was a shortage of everything. All creatures from the previous year came to life again — not one was missing! And so many new creatures were born, the whole country was swarming with them all.

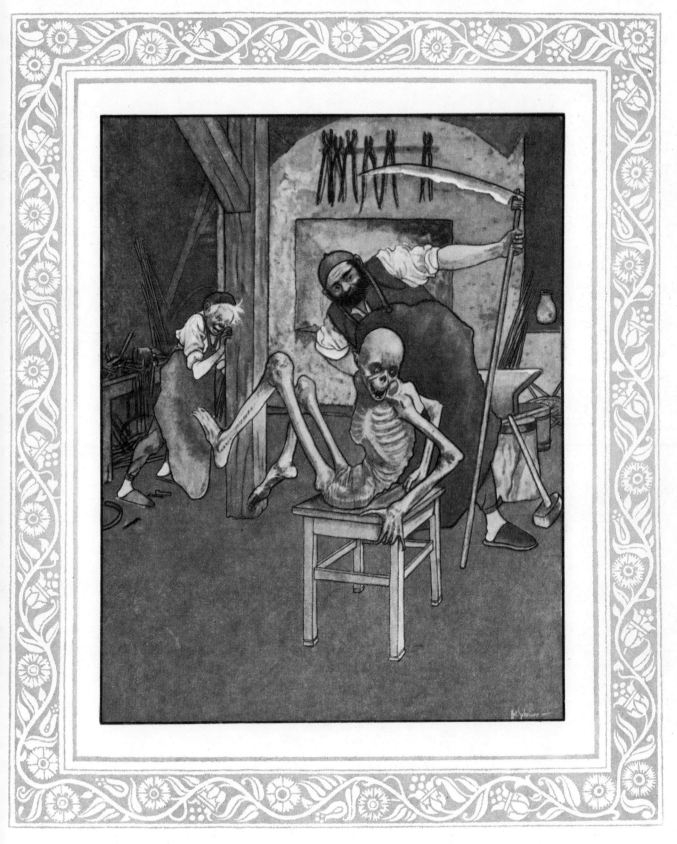

Birds, mice, insects, maggots and other pests devoured and destroyed all the crops in the fields; the meadows were stripped naked, and looked scarred as after a fire; the trees stood bare and sad, their leaves and blossom eaten up by butterflies and caterpillars — and not one of them could be killed! The lakes and rivers were so packed with fish, frogs, water spiders and other water creatures that the water stank and was not fit to drink. The sky was full of clouds of gnats, flies and midges, and the ground was thick with horrid crawling insects which would have surely bitten anyone to death, if only he was able to be killed. People staggered about, half dead, looking like shadows, unable to live, yet unable to die.

Then the blacksmith saw what misery his foolish request had brought upon the world, and he said, 'God was wise after all when he sent Death into this world!'

He returned home and gave himself up to Death and set him free. Death strangled the blacksmith at once and immediately set to work, and from that moment, slowly but surely everything returned to normal.

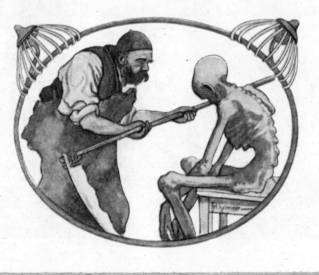

WISDOM AND LUCK

One day, Luck and Wisdom came face to face on a narrow foot bridge. 'Out of my way!' Luck cried.

In those days Wisdom was still very young and inexperienced and he did not know how to behave. 'Why should I get out of your way?' he asked. 'You're no better than I!'

'The one who achieves the most must be the better of us two,' Luck replied. 'Do you see that young peasant ploughing the field? Enter his head, and if he gets on better with your help than with mine, I shall always dutifully move out of your way whenever and wherever we meet.'

Wisdom agreed and he crept into the peasant's head. As soon as the young man felt Wisdom inside him, he began to reason. 'Am I to work this plough day in, day out until I die? There must be a better and an easier way to make a living!'

He put the plough away and rode home.

'Father,' he said, 'I am tired of farming. I'd rather learn to be a gardener.'

'Have you lost your head, Tom?' the father exclaimed, but then he thought it over and he said, 'Well, if gardening is really what you want, then go, and God go with you. Your brother will inherit the cottage when I die.'

Tom had lost the cottage, but he did not care. He went to the royal palace and found work with the king's gardener. The gardener did not have to teach him much, so quick was Tom to learn, and before long he did not even listen to the gardener's advice. He was so wise, he knew exactly what to do without being told.

The gardener was angry at first, but when he saw how much the garden had improved, he stopped grumbling and allowed Tom to work in his own way. 'You seem to be wiser than I,' he admitted.

Before very long Tom made the garden so beautiful that the king took great delight in it and often strolled along the paths with the queen and their only daughter. The princess was very beautiful, but since she was twelve years old she had not uttered a single word. This deeply grieved her father, who proclaimed that any man able to make the princess speak again would become her husband. Many young kings, princes and noblemen came and went, but not a single one had succeeded in making her break her silence.

'Why shouldn't I try my luck?' Tom thought. 'Who knows? She may reply when I start asking questions.'

Without wasting more time he went to the king who, with his counsellors, took Tom to his daughter's room. Now the princess had

a little dog, of whom she was very fond. He was a clever little dog, who seemed to understand everything she wanted of him.

When Tom came in with the king and the counsellors, he pretended not to see the princess, but turned and spoke to the little dog. 'I've heard you are very clever,' he said, 'so I want to ask your advice. I had two workmates, a wood carver and a tailor. Once, when we were travelling together through a forest, we had to sleep out. We built a big fire to keep off the wolves and kept watch in turn. The wood carver's turn came first, and as time hung heavily on his hands, he carved the form of a maiden from a tree stump. When the doll was finished, he woke the tailor, who was the next one to guard. "What is this?" he asked, seeing the big doll. "I carved her from a tree stump to help pass the time," said the wood carver. "Why don't you dress her, if you get bored." The tailor took out his scissors, needle and thread and some cloth and began to sew. When he was finished, he dressed the doll and woke me, as it was my turn to watch. "What have we here?" I asked, and he explained, "The wood carver carved the doll out of a tree stump to help pass the time. I wanted something to do, so I dressed her. If you get bored too, why don't you teach her to speak?" And truly, by morning I had taught her to speak. But when my friends woke up, they each wanted to keep the doll. The wood carver cried, "I made her!" The tailor said, "I dressed her!" And I said, "I taught her to speak!" Now tell me, little dog, to which of us does the doll belong?'

The little dog remained silent, but the princess spoke instead. 'Who else should have her but you? What good was the wood carver's doll without life? What good was she clothed but without speech? You gave her the best gifts, life and speech, so she belongs to you by right.'

'You have sealed your own fate,' Tom now cried, 'for I have given

you back your speech and a new life, so by right you belong to me.'

One of the king's counsellors then said, 'His Royal Majesty will reward you royally for loosening his daughter's tongue, but he cannot give her to you, for you are of low birth.'

The king was quick to agree. 'Yes, you are of low birth. I shall give you a rich reward instead of my daughter.'

But Tom would not hear of such a thing. 'The king made a promise, there were no exceptions. He proclaimed that the man who could make his daughter speak again would be her husband. The king's word is law. If a king expects his subjects to obey the law, he must do so himself. So the king must give me his daughter.'

'Tie him up, guards!' the counsellor cried. 'Who do you think you are to order your king about? Anyone who says that the king must do a thing is guilty of treason and must be put to death. Now, Your Majesty, please give the order to have this man's head chopped off.'

'Let him die by the sword!' said the king.

Poor Tom was bound and led to the place of execution. Luck was there, already waiting. 'See where the poor fellow has ended up with your help?' Luck whispered to Wisdom. 'He's about to lose his head! Now stand aside, and let me take over!'

The moment this was done the executioner's sword snapped in two right at the hilt — just as if someone had cut right through it. Before a replacement could be brought, a herald came galloping from the town as fast as his horse would carry him, blowing his trumpet and waving a white flag, closely followed by the royal coach, which had been sent to fetch Tom.

And this was how it came about. When Tom had been led away to his execution, the princess turned on her father. 'You were wrong, and that young man was right! A king must keep his word! And as for Tom being of simple birth, you can easily make him a prince!'

'You are right, daughter,' the king agreed. 'Let Tom be a prince!'

With that they sent their coach for Tom, and the counsellor who had provoked the king into breaking his word was executed instead.

Much later, when Prince Tom and his bride were driving from the wedding ceremony, they bumped into Wisdom; when he saw there was no way of avoiding Luck, he hung his head in shame and moved away sideways.

Ever since that day, Wisdom gives Luck a wide berth.

THE THREE WICKED FAIRIES

Once there was a boy who had no father and no mother and who was so very poor that if he were not to die of hunger he would have to find someone to feed him in exchange for his work. He walked such a long way, he knocked on so many doors, but no one wanted to take him into their service, till he came to a lonely old cottage on the edge of the forest.

In the doorway sat an old man who had only dark hollows where his eyes should have been. The goats in the shed were bleating sadly. 'You poor things,' the old man sighed, 'how I wish I could drive you to pasture! But how can I, when I cannot see, and I have no one to send in my place.'

'Send me, master,' the boy cried. 'I'll look after the goats, and I'll look after you too, if you let me!'

'What is your name?'

'They call me Ivan,' the boy replied, and he told the old man his story.

'So be it, Ivan, you can work for me. First drive the goats out to pasture. But keep away from the forest clearing, there are some wicked fairies there who would put you to sleep and then steal your eyes as they stole mine.'

'Don't worry, master,' Ivan replied, 'they are not going to get my eyes!' With that he drove the goats out to the pasture.

The first and the second day he let them graze in the nearby open meadows, but on the third day he said to himself, 'I know where there is better grass than here. Why should I be afraid of fairies?' Ivan then cut three bramble shoots off a bush, hid them in his hat and drove the goats to the forest clearing. The goats scattered and munched away, and Ivan sat down on a boulder in the shade.

Before very long, a lovely fairy appeared. She looked just like a beautiful doll, dressed all in white, with long flowing raven-black hair and sparkling black eyes. 'Good morning, little goatherd,' she cried. 'Look what lovely apples grow in our garden! I've brought one for you, so you can taste how delicious they are.' And she offered him a lovely rosy apple.

But Ivan knew that if he took the apple and bit into it he would fall asleep, and then the fairy would steal his eyes, so he said, 'Thank you, but no, lovely maiden! My master has an apple tree in his garden which yields even nicer apples than yours. I've had my fill of apples for today.'

'If you don't want it, I shan't force you,' the fairy muttered, and went away.

Shortly afterwards, another fairy came. She was even lovelier than the first and in her hand she held a beautiful red rose. 'Good morning, young goatherd,' she said. 'Look what a lovely rose I have picked for you! And it is such a fragrant bloom. See how heavenly it smells!'

'Thank you, but no, lovely maiden! My master has roses in his garden with sweeter fragrance than yours. I've smelt enough sweet-scented roses for one day.'

'If you don't want to, I shan't force you,' the second fairy snapped crossly, and she went away.

Presently a third fairy appeared, the youngest and the prettiest of them all. 'Good morning, young goatherd,' she cried.

'Good morning to you too, lovely maiden,' said Ivan.

'What a handsome lad you are,' the fairy remarked, 'but you'd be more handsome still if your hair was properly combed. Come here and I will comb it for you.'

Ivan did not say a word, but when the fairy stepped to his side, he took off his hat, took out a bramble shoot and struck her on the hand.

The fairy began to scream. 'Help, oh, help!' she cried, for she was glued to the spot with the pain. Ivan took no notice of her tears, but bound her hands with the bramble shoot.

The other fairies came running to her, and when they saw their sister thus caught and bound, they begged Ivan to untie her and set her free.

'Unbind her yourselves!' he snapped.

'Oh, we can't, we just can't! Our hands are so soft, the prickly bramble would hurt them.'

But when they realised that Ivan would not change his mind, they

went to the fairy's aid and tried to untie the bramble shoot. As soon as they were near, Ivan jumped on them, struck their hands too with the other bramble shoots and tied them up like their sister.

'Now I've got you, you wicked fairies, who stole my old master's eyes!' he cried.

Ivan ran all the way home, and he burst into the cottage, shouting, 'Master! Come with me! I've found someone who will give you back your eyes!'

He led the old man to the clearing, and said to the first fairy, 'Now tell me, where are my master's eyes? If you fail to do so, you shall be flung into the river below!'

'I don't know where they are, I truly don't,' the fairy protested.

'Then in the water you go!' Ivan cried, and was about to throw her into the fast flowing stream.

'Oh, don't throw me in, please don't!' the fairy pleaded. 'I'll give you your master's eyes!' She led Ivan to a cave where there was a big heap of eyes. There were big ones and little ones, black ones, red ones, blue ones and green ones. The fairy chose a pair and passed them to Ivan.

When Ivan inserted the eyes in his master's head, the old man was most upset. 'Oh dear, oh dear,' he wailed, 'these are not my eyes! I can see nothing but owls!'

Ivan grew angry. He picked up the wicked fairy and threw her in the river. Then he turned to the second fairy. 'Tell me, where are my master's eyes?'

This fairy, too, began to make excuses, but when Ivan threatened to throw her into the river, she led him to the cave and chose another pair of eyes.

But the old man moaned again, 'Oh dear, oh dear, these are not my eyes! I can see nothing but wolves!'

Ivan seized the second fairy and threw her into the water with such force that she went plonk! right to the bottom.

'Tell me, where are my master's eyes?' Ivan asked the third fairy, who was the youngest and the prettiest. She took him to the cave, and selected a pair of eyes, but when they were set in the old man's head, again he cried, 'Oh dear, oh dear, I can see nothing but pike!'

When Ivan realised that he had been deceived once again, he was about to drown this wicked fairy too, but she sank to her knees and begged, 'Don't drown me, dear Ivan, please don't! Spare me, and I will truly find the right pair this time!'

They were at the very bottom of the pile. When Ivan inserted them into the empty hollows, his master cried joyfully, 'These are my eyes! My very own! God be praised, I can see again at last!'

From that day on Ivan and the old man lived together in harmony and comfort. Ivan took the goats to pasture, while the old man stayed at home and made goat cheese, which they ate together at night.

And the wicked fairy, whose life they had spared, was never again seen in the forest clearing.

PETER AND HIS GOAT

Once there was a king who had an only daughter, but no one could make her laugh. She was very sad. One day, the king proclaimed that any man who could make the princess laugh would have her for his wife.

Now in this kingdom there was a certain shepherd who had an only son called Peter. When he heard what the king had promised, Peter said to his father, 'Let me try, too, father. Who knows, maybe I'll make her laugh. All I want to take with me is our goat.'

'Very well,' the father agreed, 'there is no harm in trying.'

The goat was no ordinary goat. If it was Peter's wish, anyone who touched her stuck to her like glue.

They set off along the road towards the royal town. On the way they met a man carrying his own leg across his shoulder.

'What are you doing with that leg on your shoulder?' Peter asked.

'When I put it on the ground, I jump a hundred miles,' the man explained.

'And where are you going?'

'To hire myself out as a servant,' said the man.

'Then come with me.'

They walked on till they met a man with a wooden shield in front of his eyes.

'What are you doing with that piece of wood in front of your eyes?' Peter asked.

'When I move it away,' the man replied, 'I see a hundred miles ahead.'

'And where are you going?'

'I am looking for a master. Do you want to take me?'

'Why not? Come with us.'

They walked on and presently they met a third man. He had a bottle under his arm, and instead of a cork, he had his thumb in it.

'Why do you keep your thumb in that bottle?' asked Peter.

'If I were to pull it out, what is in it spurts out a hundred miles. I can spray any objects I want. Why don't you take me into service, you may benefit, and so may we.'

'Why not? Come with us.'

By and by they came to the town where the king lived, and there they bought ribbons for the goat. They came to a tavern where the innkeeper had been told to expect them, and that he should let them

eat and drink as much as they wished, for the king would foot the bill. They tied the ribbons all over the goat's neck and asked the inn-keeper to look after her. He put the goat in the hayloft where his daughters slept.

The innkeeper had three daughters, Nora, Dora and Marta, and they were still awake. Nora said, 'Oh, how I'd love one of those pretty ribbons! I'll take one off that goat.'

'Don't do it,' Dora warned, 'They'll be able to tell it has gone.'

But Nora would not listen, and went to get herself a ribbon. No sooner had she touched it than she stuck fast to the goat. Time pas-sed, and she did not return. 'Go and fetch her,' Marta said to Dora.

So Dora went over to Nora. 'Come on, don't take any more,' she said, tapping her sister on her back. At once, she was well and truly stuck, too.

'Come along, you two!' Marta now called. 'Don't take them all!' She went over to her sisters, tugged at Dora's skirt, but as soon as she touched it, she too was well and truly stuck.

Early the next morning Peter came for the goat, and he led the lot away, Nora, Dora and Marta. The innkeeper was still fast asleep.

As they were walking through the village, the magistrate hap-pened to look out of his window. 'Good gracious!' he cried. 'That's Marta! What's going on?'

He ran out and grabbed the girl's hand to try and pull her away, and now he too was well and truly stuck. A cowherd was passing by, driving his herd to the market, and the bull brushed against the ma-gistrate and was stuck, too.

At last this strange procession arrived at the palace. The servants saw it first, and they hastened to their king and said, 'Oh, Your Ma-jesty, what a sight there is! We've had all sorts of shows and mas-querades in the past, but never anything like this!'

They brought the king's daughter out into the forecourt. The princess took one look and she burst out laughing so loudly, the whole palace shook.

Everyone crowded round Peter to find out who he was.

'I am a shepherd's son,' he replied, 'and my name is Peter.'

'This will never do,' they said. 'You are of low birth. The king cannot give you his daughter unless you prove yourself further.'

'What do you want me to do?' Peter asked.

'There is a spring a hundred miles away from here,' they said. 'Take this cup, fill it at the spring, and return here within one minute! Then the princess will be yours.'

Peter turned to the fellow with his leg upon his shoulder. 'Didn't you tell me that with your foot on the ground you could jump a hundred miles?'

'No sooner said than done,' the servant replied. He took the cup, put his foot to the ground and disappeared.

The minute was almost up and he had not returned. Peter turned to his second servant. 'You said that without your wooden shield you could see a hundred miles. Take a look and see what our friend is doing!'

'Oh, master, he is lying down. Oh, dear, he's fast asleep!'

'That's bad,' Peter muttered. 'He'll never make it in time.' Then he remembered the third servant. 'You said that if you pull your thumb out of that bottle you could splash someone a hundred miles away. Hurry and splash our man, make him wake up! And you, my sharpsighted friend, tell me if he is moving!'

'Yes, master, he is waking up, he is rubbing his eyes now, he is drawing the water.'

With one leap the first servant was back, just in the nick of time too!

The king's counsellors put their heads together and they decided that Peter would have to fulfil yet another task. Deep in the forest, they said, amongst rocks there lived a fierce unicorn that had killed many people. If Peter destroyed the beast, he would get the princess.

Peter took his friends with him and they all went to the forest. In a grove among the fir trees, three beasts were lying down. They were so heavy and big that their bodies made a hollow in the ground where they lay. Two were harmless but the third was the fierce unicorn.

Peter stuffed some stones and fir cones in his shirt and with his friends he climbed a tree directly above the beasts. Then he dropped a few stones on to the unicorn.

The unicorn turned to the beast next to it and growled, 'Leave me alone! What are you prodding me for?'

'I'm not touching you!' came the reply.

Peter let some more stones fall.

'Stop it!' the unicorn roared. 'You've done it again!'

'But I haven't touched you!' the other monster protested.

Then they pounced on each other and began to fight. The fierce unicorn tried to run its opponent through with its horn, but the beast jumped aside, and the charging unicorn ran its horn right through a tree trunk and could not pull it out.

Peter and his friends jumped from the tree, and the sight of them sent the two harmless beasts running away into the bushes. They cut off the head of the fierce unicorn and carried it back to the palace.

The counsellors were amazed at Peter's success.

'What shall we do now?' they asked each other. 'Must we give him the princess after all?'

'That can never be,' said one of the courtiers, 'such an ordinary man to marry the daughter of a king! There is nothing else for it — we must remove him from this world!'

The king then instructed his counsellors to listen carefully to whatever Peter said.

Now there was a certain old woman in the king's household and she said to Peter, 'There is an ill wind blowing today. They intend to remove you from this world.'

'I am not afraid,' Peter replied. 'Why, when I was only twelve years old I killed twelve with one blow.' This happened once when his mother had baked a cake. Twelve flies had settled on it, and he killed all twelve with one swipe.

But when the counsellors heard his words, they said, 'We will just have to shoot him.'

So they called out the soldiers and ordered them to be ready to fire, and then they told Peter a parade was being held in his honour in the forecourt of the palace. As Peter was about to walk out on to the balcony, he turned to the friend who used his thumb as a cork and he said, 'You told me that when you pull out your thumb, you can soak everything. Now go ahead and squirt!'

Out came the thumb and out gushed a fountain of water, right into the soldiers' eyes till they all turned blind and could not see a thing.

The counsellors saw that they were beaten, and with a sigh they told Peter that he could have the king's daughter. They dressed him in a gown fit for a prince and prepared for the wedding.

What a wedding it was too! There was music and singing and feasting and drinking. Everyone accepted Peter as their new prince, and he always knew how to make his princess laugh. And so they lived together in laughter and happiness for many long years.